ALSO BY JACK D. FERRAIOLO

The Big Splash

KICKS

JACK D. FERRAIOLO

AMULET BOOKS
NEW YORK

Cataloging-in-Publication Data has been applied for and may be obtained from the Library of Congress.

ISBN 978-0-8109-9803-2

Text copyright © 2011 Jack D. Ferraiolo
Book design by Chad W. Beckerman

Published in 2011 by Amulet Books, an imprint of ABRAMS. All rights reserved.

Printed and bound in U.S.A.

10 9 8 7 6 5 4 3 2 1

Amulet Books are available at special discounts when purchased
in quantity for premiums and promotions as well as fundraising
or educational use. Special editions can also be created to specification.
For details, contact specialmarkets@abramsbooks.com or the address below.

ABRAMS
THE ART OF BOOKS SINCE 1949
115 West 18th Street
New York, NY 10011
www.abramsbooks.co...

TO EMILY AND MATTHEW . . .
MY TWO LITTLE MONKEY WRENCHES

–J. F.

SIDEKICKS

1

I'M SITTING ON A FILTHY CHIMNEY,

eighty stories above street level, watching from the shadows as one of my personal top five dumbest villains tries his best to wrap his mind around a hostage situation of his own creation. His name is Rogue Warrior, and he's six feet five inches of bad skin and steroid-fueled muscles. His hostage, an attractive woman (of course, she's attractive . . . it's hard to get money for an ugly hostage), is going with the traditional "scream my way to freedom" attempt. It's not going well for either of them.

"No fancy tricks!" Warrior yells to the cops at ground level. "You get me my money, or I swear to God I'll drop her!"

Upon hearing this, Rogue's hostage finds a whole other screaming gear, one that threatens to tear a hole in any eardrum within fifty miles. I quickly size her up: five feet seven inches, one hundred thirty pounds. Dropped from this height, she'd hit the ground in less than thirty seconds.

I check the clock on the top of the building a few feet to my left. 8:45. It's time.

"Do it or she's dead!" he yells. "You hear me!"

"Of course, they don't hear you," I say, dropping from my perch. "They're eighty stories down."

"Bright Boy!" he yells, and whirls to face me.

"She's screaming like a fire alarm, and I doubt they hear her," I say.

His face scrunches up, as if he doesn't want to believe what I'm saying, but is aware enough of his own shortcomings in the brains department to know that he should. "They can hear me," he says meekly.

"No, they can't. Listen, Rogue, I know you have a problem with the whole 'planning' aspect of planning a crime, but next time you decide to do this hostage thing, you might want to choose a location where the cops can actually hear your demands. Otherwise, you might do something stupid. Like this."

"Shut up, Bright Baby. Where's your daddy, Phantom Justice? Huh?" He smiles, proud of his "joke," then looks to his hostage for some supportive laughter. All he gets is a shock-induced stare.

"I guess it's true what they say," I respond, "steroids can make you strong, but they can't make you funny."

His smile disappears. "Go ahead," he snarls, "make another crack about steroids. You and your daddy will be scraping this lady off the sidewalk with a putty knife." That wakes her up . . . and she starts screaming again.

"All right, let's just drop the tough talk and calm down," I say over her screams. Rogue Warrior is a plus/plus speed and strength like I am, but all the steroids have given him a distinct size advantage. On the other hand, he's ridiculously bulky. He may still be faster than the average person, but I'm not the average person. To me, it looks like he's moving underwater. I could hit him fifteen times before he could lift an arm to defend himself. But he's holding a hostage . . . and I'm just the sidekick. My orders are to distract, not engage.

"Ugh," I say. "Her screaming is giving me a headache."

His face breaks into a big, dumb, evil smile. It's a bully's smile. "I like it."

I feel myself getting angry, but anger isn't going to help me in this situation . . . it's only going to get in the way . . . so I push it aside. "Right. Any way you could let her go, and you and I can settle this?"

"Ha! You're kidding, right? She's my bargaining piece!"

"OK . . . so what are you asking for?" I ask.

"Five hundred million."

"Seriously?"

"Do I look like I'm joking?" he asks, shaking the woman for emphasis.

"Is she all you've got?" I ask.

"What do you mean?"

"Well, she's just a civilian, right?"

"Yeah."

"So you're nuts if you think the city's going to pony up five hundred million for someone other than a political figure or a celebrity," I say. "I mean, no offense, lady, you're really pretty, and I'm sure you're nice, and all life is sacred, blah, blah, blah . . . but come on? Five hundred million? The city can buy a bridge for that price."

"Is that so?"

"Yeah."

The bully smile creeps back onto his face. "Well . . . maybe I should just drop her, then." He swings her back over the edge. "I mean, seeing as how she ain't no good for leverage no more. Maybe all she's good for is showing the world that you and your daddy don't always win, huh? How'd you like that?" He lets go of her, then quickly grabs her again before she can fall too far. She screams, starts sobbing, pleads for her life. Rogue Warrior starts laughing. "Yeah, baby, talk to me. Tell me what you'll do for me if I let you live."

He's toying with her. I suppress the urge to take him on. He's strong and stupid, and only one of those is a weakness. Play to *his* strength and he wins. Stay patient . . . stay patient . . .

"Whoopsy!" He drops her, then quickly grabs her again. "I'm just sooo clumsy!"

She's screaming and babbling.

Out of the corner of my eye, I see one of the shadows behind Rogue Warrior shift. That's the signal.

"Hey, idiot!" I shout. "Were you born stupid, or did all the steroids make you that way?"

His jaw tightens. "What'd I say? Huh? Make another steroid crack and see what happens!"

"So, show me, Steroid Warrior! Show me what happens when a juiced-up moron like you gets angry! Come on!"

"Oh, you're gonna die, Bright Baby! But first—say

good-bye to the nice lady!" He tosses the woman over the side, like she was nothing more than an empty coffee cup. He rushes me. Even with his bulk, he's fast. Lucky for the falling woman, I'm faster. I leapfrog him, land on the building ledge, then propel myself off the side of the building. Phantom Justice's giant black cape flaps over my head, heading straight for Rogue Warrior.

"Hey! Come back here, you cowa—ooof!" Rogue Warrior's insult is cut off by Phantom's boot hitting him in the face.

"Your night of evil is over, scu—" is all I hear of Phantom's speech before I'm out of earshot. That's OK. I've heard it before, and I've got a little something else to focus on at the moment.

At this rate of descent, I only have twenty seconds left to catch up to the plummeting, screaming ex-hostage before she becomes an ex-screaming ex-woman. I straighten out my body like a diver to make myself as aerodynamic as possible, but there's still no way I'm going to be able to reach her in time. I flip open the secret compartment on my belt buckle and hit the third button from the left. Small propulsion units on the bottom of my boots click on, giving me a short burst of speed, allowing me to close the distance between us.

She's falling with her back toward the ground, eyes closed, waving her arms and legs in a futile attempt to swim back to the roof of the building. It's slowing her down a little, which is good. But now I have to do a little kung fu at 150 mph in order to avoid her flailing limbs and find a good grip on her. It's not working.

"Hey!" I yell. She opens her eyes, and just the fact that she finds herself looking at a human face in this situation startles her into stillness. I use that moment to grab her waist and pull her close. She wraps her arms around my neck and presses up against me. Her nails are digging into my back. She smells like lilacs. My heart starts pounding, and not because the street is closing in.

We pass flagpole FP-12. I reach up with my right arm as my instincts override my hormones. I feel the cold, smooth metal hit my hand; I clamp down tight enough to stop our descent, but loose enough for us to swing around. My tendons crack as our momentum carries us up and over once . . . twice. On the upswing of the second revolution, I push her off me and toss her in a high arc toward the roof of the neighboring building. She flies silently. Either she trusts me, or she's all screamed out.

I swing halfway around, then plant my feet on the flagpole and use it to push off, like it's a diving board. I zoom on a line drive, hit the roof, somersault once, then pop up sprinting. I look up over my left shoulder, just in time to see the woman heading my way. I check my footing . . . I'm running out of real estate. I look back, tracking her like a fly ball that, I hope, wasn't hit out of the park.

She hits my hands. I wrap my arms around her, then somersault twice to stop our momentum. When I pop up, she's cradled in my arms. I look down. We're two inches from the edge of the roof. I take a deep breath, then let it out slowly. Now's not the time to reveal to the panic-stricken woman how close I came to misjudging things.

I try to keep my composure, but my legs are shaking. The woman nuzzles her face into my neck. She's breathing heavily, and each breath sends a fresh set of shivers across my skin. Her blouse is torn and disheveled, and I can see the top of her bra: pink lace. Her chest is heaving up and down. Her breath is tickling the hairs on my neck.

The activity below my belt starts before I can even think to stop it. I realize what's going on and start thinking about baseball, about sharks, about world geography . . . anything to try to put the brakes on.

"That was amazing," she whispers, her lips pressed up against my ear. "You're amazing."

And there it is. Game, set, match. I'm standing at full attention. Puberty, one; self-control, zero.

All right . . . I can still get out of this with little to no damage. All I have to do is put her down and get the heck out of here. I start to lower her, but then she starts running her fingers through the back of my hair . . .

Oh God . . . What do I do now? Maybe she's really into me. But maybe she isn't? Maybe she's just being nice. Or what if she's in shock and has no idea where she is or what she's doing? But then what if she accidentally brushes against "it," and "it" totally like wakes her up? And she suddenly realizes she's gone from being thrown off a roof by a juiced-up freak to being held several stories off the ground by a teen-aged pervert wearing bright yellow tights? Oh God . . . Phantom Justice never trained me for this.

OK . . . calm down . . . deep breath . . . ignore the feeling of her fingers caressing your neck . . .

"Uhh . . . miss?" I manage to croak out.

She opens her eyes and looks up at me, dreamily. She licks her lips. "Mm-hm?"

Oh God . . .

Before I can say anything other than "Uhh," a loud *WHUP-WHUP-WHUP* fills the air, making talking impossible. A spotlight clicks on, blinding me.

"Bright Boy!" a guy on the official Channel 4 News helicopter yells. "Hey, Bright Boy!!"

Great. The news choppers never come looking for me. NEVER. They usually have all they can handle filming Phantom Justice's fights. And now, the ONE time they come looking for ME, I'm holding a beautiful, shock-addled woman and pitching a bright yellow tent. I just hope to God they've got their camera pointed above my waist.

"Hey! Bright Boy! Is that a banana in your tights, or are you just happy to be on TV?!" the cameraman yells.

Crap.

I can't hear them laughing because the helicopter is so loud, but every once in a while, one of their higher-pitched howls makes it through the noise. Plus, I can see them rolling around the floor of the chopper. For a second, the un-heroic part of me hopes they fall out. I want to see how funny they think my tights are when I'm their only hope of survival. But they don't . . . and I start to feel bad for wishing death upon them for laughing at me. Now I'm arguing with myself.

I have to get out of here.

"I have to get out of here," I say, and put the woman down.

"Mm-hm," she says in that same dreamlike way. Her knees are shaking, but they hold. Over my shoulder, I hear her say, "How do I get down?" I feel bad, but there's no way I'm picking her up again. The fire department will have to figure it out. I sprint away, leap off the building, do two rotations off FP-12, release, and soar into the air. There's a dark alley between two buildings, and I head for it.

I hit the alley, landing on a fire escape a few stories up. Thankfully, it's too dark for anyone to see me. I sit down, put my knees up, and cradle my head in my hands.

"You saved the innocent," comes an intense whisper from the fire escape above me. It's Phantom Justice. "Good job."

His costume makes him nearly impossible to see in the darkness, so I don't even bother trying. "Thanks. How'd things go with Warrior?"

"Another piece of filth off the street," he growls.

"Uhhh . . . yup." I never know what to say when he says things like that. "So, you took him down quickly, huh?"

"Yes. How did you deduce that?"

"The news copter paid me a visit. They never do that unless you're already done and, even then, they usually just fly away. Tonight, they . . ." I trail off. I really don't want to talk about what happened. Phantom isn't really listening to me, though, so it doesn't matter.

"Yes. The news. I would prefer to avoid the attention, but I realize it's necessary," he says, still using the intense whisper, even though I'm the only one around to hear him. I used to think that whisper was kind of dark and cool, but lately it's been getting on my nerves. "If we're going to be victorious in this war on the sick and depraved criminals of this city, we need to keep winning the hearts and minds of the public."

"Uh-huh."

"We need to be the face of justice."

"Yeah . . . not sure people will be focusing on my face," I mumble.

"What was that?"

"Nothing. Never mind. Are we done? Can we go home now?"

"Hm. The city is quiet. Take Sweep Route Sixteen and meet me back at the car in an hour."

I sigh. "OK."

"Remember our purpose: 'Through the darkness and the light—'" He pauses, waiting for me to recite it with him. I'm *really* not in the mood, but there's no way he's going to leave until I do.

"We'll defeat the wrongs and make them right," we finish together . . . just like we have almost every night for the past seven years. Tonight, it takes every ounce of willpower in my body to say it without rolling my eyes.

He reaches down and pats me on the shoulder. "Good soldier. One hour," he says, then takes off.

I rub my eyes with the heels of my hands and take a deep breath. After what just happened, the last thing I want to do is go back out there . . . into the city . . . where people might see me. I feel like people have seen more than enough of me already . . .

But, an order is an order.

I take another deep breath, let it out, then leap off the fire escape. The quicker I get this over with, the quicker I can get out of this stupid costume.

2

THEY KEEP SHOWING IT OVER AND OVER.

There's me catching up to the woman in midair. There's
me grabbing the flagpole, swinging around, then tossing
her in the air. There's me leaping off the flagpole, landing
on the roof, and catching the falling woman less than a
foot from the edge. It's all very impressive, and each time
I see it, I pray that they're going to stop the tape right
there after the catch. That's it. The story's done. Put the
street cleaner away. But then I hear the snickers from the
in-studio crew as the shot from the helicopter camera gets
closer, and I know that this time is going to be exactly like
the seventeen other times they've shown it. Sure enough,
the shaky shot levels off, and there I am, in close-up,
showing just how excited I am to have saved that woman.

That's when they cut back to the studio, where the female host of the early morning show, even after seeing it seventeen times, fights a losing battle with her giggles. She can't even look at the camera. The "wacky weatherman" sitting to her left is just bursting at the seams to say one of the thirty "witty" lines he must've spent all night writing. This time it's, "Well, I for one am glad to see that Bright Boy was able to *rise* to the occasion." The off-camera crew starts laughing, and then they cut to the male host, who waits a beat to deliver the punch line. "Ladies and gentlemen, we just witnessed the night that Bright Boy"—pause . . . dramatic look to the camera—"became Bright Man." Laughter, whoops, hollers, applause, then cut to commercial.

"So, you gonna listen to those idiots all morning, or are we gonna do this?" Louis asks. Louis Sullivan is our butler, trainer, confidant, and all-around voice-of-reason. He's six feet two inches tall, and about 260 pounds, with long hair and a handlebar mustache. He doesn't look particularly muscular. I mean, he's burly . . . he just looks like he's a little out of shape. Trust me. He's not.

At the moment, he's all geared up and standing in the middle of the boxing ring in Trent Clancy's in-home gym, Trent Clancy being Louis's boss, my legal guardian, and the alter ego of Phantom Justice. "Come on, we gotta leave in forty minutes and I still gotta fry up those cutlets."

Whenever I have a tough night, Louis packs my favorite lunch—a fresh chicken cutlet sandwich. It's usually still warm when I get to it. He knows that for the twenty minutes it takes for me to eat that sandwich, the only thing on my mind is the next bite.

"Fine," I say, and reach to turn the TV off.

"Naw," he says. "Leave it on."

"Why? You want to see if it distracts me?"

He smiles. "Naw. You're Bright Boy . . . big time super hero. You can't be distracted by something as little as a TV, right?"

I don't answer him. Instead, I leap, do a somersault in the air, and land in the ring. I give him my most confident, determined look, to show him that I mean business. Louis isn't looking at me. He's too busy adjusting his pads.

Louis is a norm, so he's covered in special padding that replicates the physiology of a plus/plus. I don't have to hold back; I can go at him full-force and not worry that I'm going to hurt him. Me going full-force is the only way for him to get an accurate gauge of how I'm fighting.

"You ready?" he asks, looking up at me.

A loud spike of laughter comes from the TV. I look over.

"Come on, kid. Focus."

I take a deep breath. Focusing right now is not going to be easy. But this is my time with Louis, and I look forward to it all week.

Plus, there's the possibility that I'll finally beat him.

I take another deep breath, shake my head, and get into my stance. Louis always says that even if you're not feeling confident, pretend like you are; your opponent won't know you're faking it. "OK, now I'm ready," I say. "The question is, are *you*? Because today's the day I beat you. I can feel it."

He laughs. "Big talk. You know, you've kissed this mat so many times, you should start introducing it as your girlfriend."

"Ha, ha," I say.

The rules are simple . . . the first person to subdue the other for three seconds wins, and anything in the ring—insults, dirty fighting—is fair game. We've been having these before-school sparring sessions twice a week since I was seven, and even though Louis isn't a plus/plus, I still haven't beaten him. Not once.

We circle each other. His stance is a hybrid of wrestling and Brazilian jujitsu, while I move around the ring more like a boxer, staying light on the balls of my feet. I have a speed and strength advantage, while Louis . . . well . . . Louis is Louis.

"You gonna throw that left jab," he asks, "or you just going to keep twitchin' it at me?"

I grimace, and readjust. No sense trying to throw it now. I've tried my best to remove any little signals before I throw a punch, but I still have a small one. And it doesn't matter how small it is: If it's there, Louis will see it.

He takes a lunge step toward me, so I roundhouse kick with my right foot, but he sees that coming, too. When my foot comes down, he's already on the other side of the ring, smirking.

"You're getting better," he taunts. "You only telegraphed that kick by half a mile instead of your usual mile."

He's trying to annoy me . . . distract me . . . He plays this game really well, but I'm not going to let him today.

I rush him, hit him with a couple of quick shots to the chest, but the padding absorbs them. While my body is still moving forward on the last punch, he spins to my right and gets along side me.

"Ear," he says, and pinches my right ear.

"Ow! Quit it!" I try to slap his hand away, but he's already gone. I have super-speed, and somehow he makes me seem slow. I can feel all the anger and frustration from last night start to bubble up. So much for focusing . . .

"Stop," he says.

"What?" I practically yell back.

"Get control."

"I have control!"

"Yeah. Obviously," he says, sarcastically. "Come on stop. Take a deep breath."

"Oh, and a deep breath is supposed to make it all better?" I yell. "I'm a nationwide joke right now! Do you know what that feels like?"

"Can't say that I do."

"I embarrassed myself on national television!"

"Yeah. You did."

"Oh, well great. Thanks a lot."

"What do you want me to say?" he asks. "You want me to lie to you?"

"Maybe you could at least muster a 'Hey, it's not that bad.'"

"Would that change anything?"

"It might," I say, even though I know it wouldn't.

"Oh, so that would stop those people on TV from laughing at your picture right now?"

His eyes shift to the TV for half a second, but I refuse to look over. I can't tell if this is a sincere discussion, or if Louis is just trying to distract me. If he is, it's a pretty cheap shot. Then again, we are in the ring . . . and in the ring, there's no such thing as a cheap shot.

And now *not* looking at the TV is as distracting as looking at it, because either way, it's all I'm thinking about.

I turn my head and look at the TV.

That was a mistake.

"Ear," he says, and tweaks my ear again.

"Ow! Why are you being such a jerk?"

"Because we're in the middle of a fight, and all you're concerned about is what those idiots on TV think of you. You're lucky I'm not a villain, kid. If this was a street fight, you'd be dead right now . . . twice. In the ring, you're supposed to have one thing on your mind, and one thing only: me."

"Fine," I bark. "You're on my mind, OK? Is the lecture over now?"

Louis pauses, looking at me with contempt. "Forget it. You wanna have that kinda attitude, find someone else to train you. I'm through." Louis turns his back to me and walks over to the corner of the ring.

At first, I don't know what to do. Does he mean he's through for the day, or through for good? Then I realize I don't care. He's still being a jerk, I'm still angry, and we're still in the ring . . . and when we're in the ring, there's no such thing as fighting dirty. I rush him.

He still has his back to me. I'm about to hit him when, at the last second, he ducks. I miss him by a fraction of an inch. When I turn back to him, he's smiling.

"All right!" he says sincerely. "That's what I want to see."

"Cheap shots?"

"Come on, kid. We've been over this. This isn't a high school football game or a spelling bee. In your line of work, there's no such thing as a cheap shot."

I give him a half smile.

"Plus, take away cheap shots and you'd have no shot at winning at all," he says, then laughs and walks to the other side of the ring.

I speed over to him. I'm still smiling, but I want to make him eat that laugh. Unfortunately, my anxiousness puts me a little off balance. Louis does a simple little sweep kick (actually more of a trip than a kick) and suddenly, I'm tumbling past him. I spring back up quickly and dive at him, but once again, I'm off-balance. Louis uses my momentum to carry me up and over. In half a second, I'm on my back with Louis's knees on my shoulders and his hands under my chin. My strength and speed mean absolutely nothing in this position. I have no leverage. I'm squirming, but it's not accomplishing anything; my body is moving around, but he has my head.

"One, two, two-and-a-half, two-and-three-quarters . . . three." Louis lets go and stands up. I don't move. I just lie there on the mat, staring up at the ceiling.

"A couple of more seconds and I could've gotten out of that," I protest feebly.

"Riiiight," he says. "So, what have we learned here today?"

I sigh. "That speed and strength don't mean anything without good technique," I say as if reading a cue card.

"And?"

"Cheap shots are good, but not always effective."

"And?"

"I can't always tell when you're testing me or just being a jerk."

Louis leans over so that his face is in my line of sight. "Yeah, I know . . . it sucks. But it's my job, y'know? I gotta get inside your head, and then pick at the things that bother you. It's the only way to keep you sharp."

"Yeah . . . I know . . ."

"There's jackals all around you, Scott. They're gonna pick you apart, they're gonna call you names and laugh at you for every little mistake you make. And you're human, so of course it's gonna get to you. And they'll use that to distract you, to make you emotional. And what happens when you fight while distracted and emotional?"

"I lose."

"Badly. I don't enjoy what I gotta do to you, but I know I gotta do it, because I don't like to think about what might happen to you if I don't." Suddenly his eyes get a little glassy, as if he might be tearing up a bit. I look away. I can't watch Louis get emotional, especially after the night I've had. Just the thought of him being upset enough to actually cry is threatening to send me right over the edge. I think he realizes this, because when I sneak a peek back at him, his usual mildly amused expression has returned. "All right . . . I think that's enough for today," he says gruffly.

I pick myself up off the mat and start walking for the ropes.

"Whoa, wait a second," he says. "Where's my prize?"

"Oh, come on . . . seriously? Every time?"

"Every time you lose. And don't pretend like you wouldn't do the same to me."

He's right. I would do the exact same thing . . . if I ever actually won, that is.

"Fine," I say, and roll my eyes.

"Come on. Nice and loud."

"Louis Sullivan is the best fighter in the whole, wide world," I say loudly, but with as little enthusiasm as possible.

"And?"

"And he makes the best pancakes ever, in the history of pancakes."

"Now *that* part of my job, I enjoy," he says.

Half an hour later, I'm in the kitchen, freshly showered and dressed in my school uniform (khakis, white shirt, navy blue sweater with an important-looking-but-meaningless crest over my heart). I'm picking half-heartedly at Louis's famous pancakes while watching the same morning crew from before find new reasons to laugh at my picture.

"If it bothers you so much, why don't you turn it off?" Louis asks as he bustles around the kitchen, putting the finishing touches on my lunch.

"I guess I keep hoping that the next time they'll stop the tape after I save the woman."

"Yeah, not likely. Look, kid, sorry to say it, but you

saving some random woman isn't news anymore. You giving a 'below the belt salute' is."

"Don't you think that's pretty pathetic?" I ask.

Louis just shrugs. "It is what it is," he says.

"What does that even mean, 'It is what it is'?" I snap.

Louis looks at me. "It means that the world is full of people that nobody cares about. That woman you saved? Nobody, outside of her family and friends, knows or cares about her. So why would people care that you saved her? Just another anonymous person they'll never meet. But you on the other hand . . . they know you."

"No, they don't."

"Yeah, they do. They watched you grow up from some cute little kid taking out bad guys three times his size—"

"—to some teenager wearing tights two sizes too small," I say.

"Well . . . yeah. You're a celebrity, kid. No one wants to hear about all the people you save. They already know that about you. They want to hear about your faults. In other words, it is—"

"—what it is. Got it. Doesn't mean I have to like it."

"Nobody said you did."

I sigh. "At least admit that I need a new costume."

Louis pauses. "Yeah," he finally agrees.

"Trent won't ever go for it, will he?"

"He might," he says, without meeting my eyes. "Now come on. You're gonna be late for school."

Louis doesn't say much as he drives me to school, which is good, because I'm not much in the mood for conversation. I know today's going to be a disaster, and I'm trying my best to mentally prepare for it. The bottom line is that I need a new costume. I'm not a kid anymore. I can't keep running around the city in neon yellow tights. They're embarrassing. In fact, the whole outfit—tights, red cape, and mask—is embarrassing. But how do I convince Trent? I've already tried a million times, and I don't have a ton of hope for the millionth-and-first time.

I also can't help thinking about what Louis said earlier, about saving the woman not being a story anymore. He's right. It's starting to feel like the public just assumes that Phantom and I are going to save the day. I mean, we still make the news when we take out some jewel thieves, or stop some plus/plus idiot from throwing a bank teller off a building, but the public just doesn't seem as "in love" with us as they used to be. Maybe Phantom and I are just the victims of our own success. We always win. We've become predictable.

Louis pulls up to Harbinger Preparatory School, the

most exclusive school in New York City. The brass plaque in front proclaims that the school was built in 1910, but with its ivy-covered stones, the place looks like it's been here forever and they built the rest of Manhattan around it. A bunch of kids are gathered outside, waiting for the day to start. It's a sea of plaid and khaki, of laughing, chatty, good-looking faces. Every morning looks like a cover shoot for the school brochure.

Harbinger is the perfect place for me to go to school. My classmates are the sons and daughters of celebrities and dignitaries. It's the kind of place where, even if everyone knew I was Bright Boy, I might not stand out. As it is now, I've turned not standing out into an art form.

"You got anything going on after school today?" Louis asks as he pulls over to the curb. "Maybe a club meeting or something?"

I give him a sarcastic smile. "Do I ever?"

He smiles back. "Nah . . . but I keep thinking that one of these days you're gonna get sick of talking to just me."

"What do you mean 'one of these days'?"

"All right. That's it. Get out of my car."

"Hey, maybe I'll join the fashion designers club," I

say as I climb out. "Maybe *they* would make me a new costume."

Louis pauses. "Do you want me to talk to Trent?" he asks.

"Really?"

"Yeah, but I can't promise anything. You know how he feels about it . . . says it makes you an icon."

"Yeah, I know. Except it's also making me a joke."

"I'll see what I can do."

"Thanks, Louis." I'd hug him, but I don't want to risk going from "invisible guy" to "parking lot hugger guy."

"Good-bye, kid," Louis says, then shoots me a wink and drives off.

I head for the school entrance, feeling a little better than I did before. The welcome chime hasn't sounded yet, so most kids are still hanging around outside. I haven't even gone three steps when I hear the laughter.

"Did you *see* him?"

"Forget him! Did you see *it?*"

"Oh my God! It was—"

"I know! How can he—"

"I know!" They all laugh.

I put my head down and walk. I try to tell myself

that they're not laughing at me, but I know that's not true. They are—they're just not laughing at the me who's in front of them right now.

Inside the scene is the same. EVERYONE is talking about my "issues" from last night. Harbinger is a K–12 school, so it's good to know that my ridicule is universal across all age groups. Even the kindergartners, the one group left that still looked up to me, seem sad and confused.

"HA! What a freak!" some girl yells.

"Total perv!" a guy says, then breaks into a series of snorting laughs.

"I know, right?!" comes the response from someone in the crowd.

"So gross!" another kid chimes in.

As I'm walking to my locker, some kid runs past me holding the front page of the newspaper over his head. "Bright Balls!" he yells. The whole hall-way erupts in laughter. I rub my eyes. Gonna be a long day . . .

It wasn't always like this. When I first started out as Bright Boy six years ago, every kid in school would have traded places with me in a heartbeat. I was Bright Boy! Sidekick to Phantom Justice! I had super-speed, super-strength, and a whole bunch of cool gadgets! I knocked the snot out of criminals! And I had the coolest costume! All the girls thought I was cute; all the boys thought I was awesome.

I used to get a huge thrill from this, being the main topic of conversation without anyone even knowing I was listening. I used to take in all of this adoration from a distance, not wanting to get close to anyone for fear that they might discover my true identity. Also, I just loved knowing that I had this giant secret. I could listen in on everyone as they shared fantasies about being Bright Boy, or becoming friends with Bright Boy, and having no idea that Bright Boy was right there, standing next to them.

A lot of things were different then. For starters, we weren't called plus/pluses like we are now; we were called supers, and there were a lot more of us around. For some reason, the name *supers* made us more lovable to the public. I'm not sure why. Maybe it's because supers sounds so heroic, while plus/plus sounds so cold and mathematical.

Then, several years back, a national scientific journal ran a report called "Science of the Supers: Explaining the Extraordinary." The basic gist of it was that scientists believe we have some slight variations to our DNA that allow us to use more of our body's potential than regular humans.

The reports said that we can have one of three extra abilities that they labeled pluses: strength, speed/reflexes, and intelligence. Having one plus is most common; in some very rare cases people have two, like me and Phantom Justice. But there has never been a documented case of someone having all three.

The scientists believe that plus speed is at top potential from day one, so I'm not going to get any faster as I get older. Plus strength is different. I'm as strong as about five full-grown men right now. Supposedly, when I turn thirty, I'll max out at fifteen men. Plus intelligence, which is the least common, works the same way: Older equals smarter. I'm not friends with any plus intelligences to know if that's true or not. The only one I even know of is a villain, Dr. Chaotic, and it's not like he and I are meeting up to have long talks over ice cream.

So being a plus/plus hero used to be awesome, but the past few years, things started to change. First of all, the plus/plus population started to dwindle, and no one was sure why. Phantom's theory is that the supers that disappeared either got "seduced from their responsibilities by the peace of a normal life" or became "cowards who succumbed to the fear of evil." I've looked on the Internet for information, but it's mostly just people with crackpot theories. One guy thinks that most of the pluses moved underground, formed a hidden network, and are now trying to root out some great evil. Another guy thinks that all the pluses are actually aliens, and the ones who disappeared were just "called home."

But really, my own hero image had been changing for a while; I just hadn't noticed. The younger kids were still huge fans of Bright Boy, but everyone else from third grade up made fun of him . . . me. They laughed at the outfit. They started thinking of him/me as a freak of nature (and not in a good way).

The less popular my Bright Boy persona got, the more I realized that my Scott Hutchinson persona wasn't very popular, either. I wasn't hated or anything; I just didn't have any close friends. I sat with a set of kids at lunch, but they were all kids who didn't quite fit into school. We got along as long as no one said much, or really made eye contact.

I realized that the years of avoiding sports teams, extracurricular activities, birthday parties, and even simple invitations to "come over and play" had made me invisible to my classmates. Somewhere along the line, they started to realize that I was always going to say no—to everything—and so they just stopped asking.

And I had been so busy, that I hadn't even noticed.

Not that it mattered, anyway. Even if I had a close friend, I'd never really be able to share things with them. I wouldn't be able to have them over to Trent's house. I'd always have to run off at a moment's notice. I couldn't risk someone getting close to me and discovering who I really am. It would jeopardize everything Trent and I work for, not to mention endanger norms like Louis who are close to us. Sure, Louis can take care of himself, but that doesn't mean I want to make him hostage bait to all of our enemies.

I don't have anything in common with my classmates, anyway. They talk about movies and TV shows I haven't seen, or music that I haven't listened to . . . I don't even know what I'm interested in, besides running around the city at night and smacking bad guys around. So really, there's no sense in trying to have friends. I'll just wait until I'm older. Maybe when you're an adult, these things don't matter as much.

"Well, lookee who we have here . . . If it isn't Snot Hutchinson!"

Oh man . . . I was so lost in thought that I wasn't scoping the hallway, and now I have to deal with Jake Berkshire and his three goons.

"Hello, Snot!" Jake says with mock enthusiasm. His friends laugh, as if changing my name from Scott to Snot is the funniest thing any of them has ever heard. Jake and his friends are a few years older than me, but we're in the same grade. I wouldn't say they're as dumb as a bag of hammers, but only because that would be an insult to the hammers.

"I said, hello, Snot." They all cackle again. Jake and his friends are the only kids in school who actually notice me, and they don't seem happy about it.

"I have to get to class," I say as meekly as I can, but I'm having a hard time mustering the energy to pretend I'm scared of them today.

"Awww . . . poor, wittle Snot has to get to class," Jake says. The idiots chime in with their own "Awwws." Jake's face gets hard and mean all of a sudden. "You'll go where I tell you to go, when I tell you to go there, got it?" He gives me a shove. Part of me doesn't want to budge, but then I'm afraid Jake'll dislocate his elbow . . . so I let my shoulder go limp and roll with it. His friends then follow suit and push me around. So far, I'm controlling the urge to knock them all out, but it's getting harder with each shove.

Things are about to escalate when Shane, one of the idiot friends, notices Dr. White, the foreign languages teacher, coming around the corner. "Jake! Teach!" he whispers loudly.

Jake, like the weasel he is, gets a panicked look on his face. I can't believe that my "bully" is scared to death of a teacher. It makes it so hard to fake taking him seriously. "See you around, Snot," he says, then knocks the books out of my hands as a parting shot. I let him, but only because if I didn't, he'd probably break his hand.

I manage to grab my books and slip into my first period social studies class right before the chime sounds. Three girls walk in after me: Olivia Duchamp, Allison Mendes, and Charlene O'Malley. They're giggling about whatever it is that girls my age giggle about, and Mr. Privet tells them to quiet down, but he's got a smile on his face, as if he doesn't really care that they're giggling. And why should he? Olivia, Allison, and Charlene are model students: pretty, smart, popular without being stuck-up, walking the tightrope between good student and teacher's pet.

I've tried to build up the courage to walk over and talk to them, but it just hasn't happened yet . . . which is ridiculous considering what I build up the courage to do every night. I mean, really, it's not like one of them is going to throw me off a building or blast me with a laser. The messed-up thing is, it might be easier for me to talk to them if I thought they might. But they're just regular girls . . . and what the heck can I say to regular girls? "Hi, I'm Scott! Any of you girls looking to hang out with a guy who can't tell you much about himself, who you can't count on for anything, who may be completely incommunicado for long stretches of time. I'll hardly ever be able to go anywhere or do anything! I'll agree to meet you places and then stand you up and not be able to give you a reason! Doesn't that sound awesome?"

Before I have a chance to pull my laptop out of my bag, the intercom statics to life. Everyone else in class pauses, too, to see if it's them getting called out of class. "Scott Hutchinson, please report to the front desk. Scott Hutchinson."

I get up from my seat and walk toward the door as everyone else goes about their business. No one looks up at me. Even Mr. Privet doesn't miss a beat. He's already into the lesson before I reach the hallway. That's another reason this school is so perfect for me . . . kids of politicians and entertainers are always getting pulled out of school for one reason or another, so they don't even blink when it happens to me.

I find myself walking pretty quickly toward the front

desk . . . almost, but not quite, slipping into a bit of plus speed. It's funny . . . even with all my concerns over being a social outcast, I still can't wait to get out of here and become Bright Boy again.

I just wish I had a better costume.

I PUT IN THE SECURITY CODES AND ENTER

the Fortress, the official secret hideout of Phantom Justice and Bright Boy. It sits underground, about a thousand feet below Trent's mansion. To tell you the truth, I'm not really sure why we even need the Fortress. It's full of all this crime-fighting equipment that Trent bought, that we never really use. The only thing we do use is the MCC, or Main Crime Computer, and that thing is a couple of years old now. I'm pretty sure I can do on my phone ninety percent of what the MCC does.

I walk past the costume room and the armory, past the revolving platform that the Stealth Phantom is parked on, and there he is—Trent Clancy, aka Phantom

Justice, standing with his back to me, staring up at the giant, wall-size monitor. Even in civilian clothes, he's impressive. Six feet three inches, 220 pounds of solid muscle, Trent is plus/plus, speed and strength, like me. Even just standing there in civilian clothes, looking up at the giant monitor, I could feel his intensity. His posture is intense. His hair is intense. If I could see his face, I bet it would have an intense look on it. And when he speaks, his voice is intense.

"Dr. Chaotic escaped from prison this morning."

Several pictures of Dr. Chaotic pop up on the monitor, in various forms of dress and disguises.

"Dr. Chaotic. Real name: unknown. Known Aliases: Richard Fairweather, Harold Riesling, James Conant. Former Location: San Raphael Maximum Security Prison. Current location: unknown. Attributes: plus intelligence. Dr. Chaotic is quite possibly the most intelligent human on the planet. Although lacking plus speed or strength, Chaotic has the ability to create and implement an unlimited amount of armor and weaponry. These devices are highly sophisticated. They enhance his physical attributes to near plus capacities, and are often capable of massive destruction. Threat level: highest." Trent recites the information from memory, as if he's reading from a case file. Unfortunately, he talks like this a lot.

"How did this happen?" I ask.

"They're not sure. They're still piecing together the details, but it appears that he constructed a small laser out of wood, a battery pack, and circuitry from an old television."

"You're kidding."

Trent turns and gives me an intense look. "No. I'm not."

I sigh. "No, I know . . . it's just an expression."

Trent continues to stare at me for a couple of uncomfortable beats, then finally turns back to the monitor.

"It took him a little more than three weeks," he says.

"That's it? Holy crud."

Trent turns again, this time with a stern look. He doesn't like it when I use words like *crud,* even though it's not a swear word, and even when it's in response to news that our most dangerous foe escaped from prison.

"Sorry."

Trent glares at me for a moment too long again, then turns back to the monitor. "He's been in prison for five years. The method of his escape suggests that he could have left whenever he wanted. So why now?" Trent asks.

He's not necessarily asking me; he's asking the room, and himself. My job is to answer, so he can get the answers that are obviously wrong out of the way. "Because he had the opportunity?"

"Someone who can make a laser out of wood and an old TV is going to have a lot of opportunities," he responds.

"Good point. It could be anything."

"Yes. Looks like we're going to have to wait until he makes the first move," he says, like he's not happy about it. "He had a sidekick, correct? Plus/plus, speed and strength, like us. Code-named—"

"Monkeywrench," I say, and shudder. I hadn't thought of him in years, and not because he wasn't memorable. I had purposely blocked him. What a weasel. Unfortunately, when we caught Dr. Chaotic, Monkeywrench had gotten away. I would've loved to see that little jerk go to jail, too.

"Monkeywrench. Right." Trent quietly looks at the monitors. His shoulders sag a bit, something I've never seen before.

"Are you OK?" I ask.

"Yes."

"You don't seem OK."

Trent takes a deep breath. "Dr. Chaotic almost killed me last time."

"Yeah, but he didn't."

"Because I got lucky."

I nodded. Trent wasn't trying to be modest. The last time we faced off against Dr. Chaotic, Trent got destroyed.

Five years ago, Champion Motor Company was working on a project code-named Destiny. They had developed a car with a special motor that could get eighty miles per gallon, without using hybrid technology. Pretty cool, right? It got even cooler. Destiny was also capable of going zero-to-sixty in under four seconds. The thing hauled. Other companies were developing similar cars, but Champion was poised to get there first. That's when Dr. Chaotic and Monkeywrench tried to step in.

Dr. Chaotic knew that all the companies competing for the pole position in the fuel economy race would do whatever they needed to do to get those plans. So, his plan was pretty straightforward: Steal the plans and sell them to the highest bidder.

Their first crime was at Champion's headquarters. Chaotic and Monkeywrench managed to get the plans out of the building, but Champion had just installed a state-of-the-art security system, which managed to stall Chaotic and Monkeywrench long enough for Phantom and me to get there. We battled them on the roof of the Champion building for half an hour before they escaped . . . without the plans. That's because as they were making their escape in Dr. Chaotic's helicopter, I managed to snag the plans away from Monkeywrench. Sure, I almost plummeted 1,500 feet to my death, but seeing the look on that little weasel's face after snatching those plans from him was totally worth it.

After that, Champion split the Destiny plans up, and hid parts of them all over the city. Dr. Chaotic and Monkeywrench spent the whole rest of the summer searching for them. They managed to snag a few, but more often than not, Phantom Justice and I were able to thwart them. They did, however, always manage to escape capture. I guess the frustration was getting to them, because by the end of August, their robbery attempts were getting more reckless, more dangerous. Then, in the last week of August, things came to a head.

Dr. Chaotic decided to stop looking for the plans and start looking for the one working prototype of the car. He figured that if he could get his hands on the prototype, he'd be able to auction that instead of the plans. He and Monkeywrench found it in a warehouse on the docks, hidden in a large crate marked Coffeemakers.

By the time we arrived, Monkeywrench had already hooked up the prototype to Dr. Chaotic's helicopter (which, even I'll admit, is pretty impressive for an eight-year-old). Monkey-boy and I started fighting as Phantom Justice tried to pull the helicopter down all by himself. Chaotic had modded the copter with some jet turbines, so it almost ripped Phantom's arms out of their sockets. Phantom then switched to Plan B, which was to lodge the car in the doorway of the warehouse. Chaotic's copter couldn't take off with the car anchoring it to the ground, but he was too stubborn to leave without it. He gunned the engines, hoping he had enough juice to break the car free. He didn't. His helicopter slammed into the ground, exploding on impact.

Dr. Chaotic managed to escape the wreckage but not without taking major damage. Phantom Justice had him cornered when Chaotic pulled out a new weapon, something he said he had been saving for just such an occasion. It was brand-new—so new that he didn't even have a name for it yet. Chaotic said it was supposed to target the unique biological makeup of a plus/plus, and somehow short-circuit their nervous system . . . or something. We still don't know if it worked the way he intended, because the thing exploded.

Monkeywrench and I were fighting a short distance away. Dr. Chaotic had just cackled evilly and proclaimed himself the victor against Phantom Justice then he pulled the trigger. The weapon exploded. I knew it was a small-blast radius, because Monkeywrench and I were fighting about thirty yards away, and we only went into minor convulsions. Phantom Justice and Dr. Chaotic had been standing only a few feet away from each other, and they were having full-blown seizures.

After that point, the night got a little hazy for me. I remember abandoning my fight with Monkeywrench. I remember feeling a surge of adrenaline, grabbing both Dr. Chaotic and Phantom Justice, and just hauling to the hospital. I remember the doctors meeting me outside and taking over. I remember leaving the hospital and rocketing through the city, thinking that I HAD to find Monkeywrench and arrest him before Phantom woke up, or Phantom was going to be angry. I remember waking up on the fire escape of an abandoned building the next morning, not sure if the events from the night were real or just a vivid dream. I went to the hospital to find out.

Dr. Chaotic was there, dazed, but healthy. He was under heavy security, and heading to jail when he fully recovered. No one knew anything about Monkeywrench; it seemed that he had just cut and run. Phantom Justice had checked himself out. I went home and slept for the next thirty-six hours. Trent slept for three days. When he finally came out of his room, he looked shaken, a little weak, but pretty much OK. It took him a couple of days to get back up to full strength. Luckily for the city, and us, there wasn't a major crime for a week or so after that.

Trent hasn't talked about it again until today. He hasn't had to. Chaotic's been in prison.

"And now he's out," Trent says. "The one man who made me feel fear, down to the core of my being."

"Uh-huh."

"He will not have that power over me. Justice has no weaknesses . . . I will not feel fear again."

"OK . . . sure," I say. "Listen, speaking of not wanting to feel certain . . . uhh . . . feelings, did Louis talk to you."

He looks annoyed, as if I'm interrupting something. "About what?"

"About my uhh . . . costume?"

"Yes." I wait for him to say something else, but he doesn't.

"Oh . . . well . . . have you seen the news?" I ask.

"Yes."

"OK . . . uhh . . . well . . ." I stammer, trying to fill in the big, uncomfortable space. "I don't think my costume fits me anymore."

"We'll get you a larger size."

"That's not what I meant. Well, I mean, it's part of what I meant. But the other part is that I don't really like it anymore."

"Oh." He continues to stare at me.

"It's just REALLY bright."

"Your name is Bright Boy."

"No, I know . . . It's just, do we have to be so obvious about it? You did see the news, right?"

"Yes, and I wanted to talk to you about that. I know you're at 'that age' . . ."

I take a deep breath, and ready myself for what kids at school always called "the talk." Really, Trent should have given me "the talk" a couple of years ago, but he always found a way to put it off. Not like I really needed him to give it to me . . . I mean, I've had three classes on the subject, and whatever wasn't covered in there, Louis filled me in on. So, Trent's pretty late to the party.

"I know it can be . . . awkward," Trent continues.

"But we are heroes . . . trying to uphold an image. And we just can't allow something like that to happen again. It's impure, and I won't allow it."

"Uh, what?" I ask, not sure I heard him correctly.

"People are going to think you're one of those perverts if every time you save someone, you have a . . . reaction."

"But . . . I couldn't . . . It's not like I meant to have an—!"

"That isn't the point, Scott. The point is that our job is to clean this city of the filth, not become dirty ourselves."

"But—"

"We wear costumes as symbols of justice to the criminals who prey on the weak," he says. "We don't wear costumes because it 'turns us on.'"

"But . . . it doesn't! I just—"

"Look . . . you screwed up . . . I'm trying to be understanding about it. Just don't let it happen again."

"Then get me another costume!"

"Scott, I don't think the costume is the problem. The problem is that you need to learn to control yourself."

My mouth hangs open. I have no idea what to say. I can't decide if I want to yell at him, or curl up into a ball and hide under a table for the rest of my life. Before

I can make my choice, the computer starts beeping. Our computer is wired into every alarm system in the city (and some we installed ourselves), so when it starts beeping, something is going down.

"Alarm at 4357 West Salem Street," Trent says. "Computer . . . Close-up." The computer gives a close-up of the alarm site on the city map. "That's IGO Computer corporate headquarters!" Trent says. "Come on . . . let's suit up."

He sprints off.

I stand there trying to process what happened. Did my mentor really just call me a pervert? And then ask me to dress the part? And still blame it all on me? And somehow leave me wondering if he's right?

"Come on, Scott," he calls. "The city awaits . . ."

I stagger along behind him, feeling angry and confused and embarrassed and guilty all at the same time. I have no idea how I'm going to put that costume on now, let alone roam around the city in it. It's going to be hard to fight with my hands blocking "the view" the whole time.

4

PHANTOM DOESN'T LIKE TO TALK

in the car; he needs that time to get into character, to "purge himself of the light and whimsy of Trent Clancy . . . to become a creature of darkness that preys on the evil of man . . . the scourge of the wicked . . . Phantom Justice!" Trust me, those are his words, not mine.

I stare out the window, listening to the twin-jet turbines of the Stealth Phantom, feeling more underdressed than ever. I wish for some sort of cataclysmic event—a system malfunction, a wrong turn into the river, a nuclear explosion—anything so I don't have to get out of the car.

"We're here," Phantom growls.

"OK. No need to be angry about it," I say.

He turns and stares at me. "Less jokes, more focus."

Why's he being such a jerk?

We park in an alley on the side of the building. Phantom cuts the engines and we get out. Everything is quiet; nothing seems out of the ordinary. This can only mean one thing. Phantom and I look at each other, then look up the side of the building. The roof. Super-criminals always head to the roof.

Our hydraulic grappling hooks zip us forty-five stories in twenty seconds. Phantom's cape flaps above me, flowing around him like a large, inky shadow. My little red cape flaps weakly against my back. We land in our battle stances, the ones that make us look like we're posing for an action figure box. We're ready for anything . . . except for what we find.

There's no one there.

In the past five years, Phantom and I have landed on hundreds of roofs to face off against hundreds of villains, but this feels different . . . like the air is charged with electricity. There's an uncomfortable buzz in the pit of my stomach. My mouth is dry. My palms are damp with sweat, so I wipe them on the front of my shirt. It doesn't help.

"Be careful," Phantom says.

I start to answer him when something slams into the side of my head. I backflip out of my tumble and spring up to see what hit me.

"Hello, Banana Pants!" comes a high-pitched voice, the same voice I remember from five years ago. Ugh. It's Monkeywrench. Apparently, in those five years, he ditched the full-face monkey mask and skin-tight black bodysuit. He's wearing a Kabuki-style monkey mask that cuts off at the nose, and a black leather-and-mesh outfit that isn't dorky or revealing at all. In fact, he looks really cool. Dammit.

"It's been a while," he squeals. "Did you miss me? Let's see . . ." His eyes drop from my face to my tights. "Hm. Apparently not. Ha-ha-ha-ha-ha!"

The little jerk went right for the jugular, and I highly doubt that was his last comment on the subject.

"Hello, Weaselwrench," I say, trying to counter.

"Weaselwrench? Is that the best you can come up with?"

He's right. *Weaselwrench* sucks.

I start to make a comment about his voice not changing yet, but I'm suddenly drowned out by a jet engine–like sound. It's Dr. Chaotic . . . flying. He's wearing a set of propulsion boots and pointing a complex-looking weapon at us.

"Well, well, well . . . if it isn't Phantom Justice," Chaotic says.

Phantom Justice's eyes narrow into slits.

"You're too late!" Chaotic yells. "I already have what I came for! And now, I'll blah, blah, blah—" Chaotic starts going on and on in a rant involving (in no particular order): his superiority to Phantom Justice (I'm not even on his radar); his belief that we are fascist slaves to the corrupt corporate system; then back to his superiority to Phantom Justice. I keep my eyes on Monkeywrench, who, frankly, looks like he doesn't know what to do with himself. To be fair, Chaotic's rant is going on a little long. After five years, I guess they're both a little rusty.

Just as Dr. Chaotic seems to be running out of gas, a news helicopter comes buzzing onto the scene. Dr. Chaotic is momentarily distracted, and that's when Phantom throws his *shuriken*. Even distracted, Chaotic is able to use his laser to knock out most of the small blades. Two get through and manage to hit one of his boots. The boot starts to spark and sputter, so Chaotic lands on the roof of the building. Cybernetic armor forms around his body.

"Just a little something to even the score," he says, sneering.

Phantom Justice starts walking toward him. "It doesn't matter what you do," he says in his trademark growl, "or what you wear, I will bring you . . . to justice!!"

"Come on!" Chaotic yells, then fires laser blasts from each of his armored forearms. Phantom sidesteps them, like walking in between raindrops, and closes in. He throws a punch. Chaotic gets his force field up, but a little late. The blow sends him sliding back ten feet.

"Heck of a fight, isn't it," comes the screechy voice of Monkeywrench, right before he punches me in the jaw. I manage to roll with it, making the punch more of a glancing blow than the knockout it was supposed to be. It does wake me out of spectator mode, though.

"Whoopsy," I say. "Looks like someone's a little slow and out of practice."

He throws a couple more punches, but I avoid them easily.

"Didn't you work out while Chaotic was away in prison?" I ask. "Hopefully, you kept your legs in shape . . . you know, so when he goes down again, you can run and hide like you did the last time."

"Ha! Idiot!" Monkeywrench is trying to laugh me off, but I can tell I got to him. He double flips toward me, then flips again and tries to connect with a windmill kick to the head. I sidestep, then send a flurry of jabs at his head; he sidesteps all but the last one. His head snaps back. I try to capitalize on it with an uppercut, but he's too fast. He slides past me and tries a sidekick to the head. I block, then grab his foot, and twist. He twirls midair and kicks out, landing on the ground as if I just ordered him to drop and give me twenty push-ups. He gets a back-kick away toward my stomach. It hits me, but I push myself back to lessen its impact. It barely hurts, only knocking the wind of me for a couple of seconds. By the time I look up again, he's facing me, in a fighting pose, ready to go again.

"Had enough?" he asks.

"You're kidding, right? Maybe you were the strongest little weasel in your 'amateur cowards fight club,' but you're back in the pros now."

"You need shorter insults," he says. "And looser pants."

I feint a left jab; he ducks right; I roundhouse kick and catch him in the face. I send another, but he avoids it and comes in with a left hook, but it's a little slow. I duck under and give a double punch to the stomach. It knocks him back.

"You used to be a decent fighter, Weasel. What happened?" I ask.

"Well, while you were growing out of your tights, I was off living a normal life. Remember a normal life? Probably hard to remember something you never had."

"What's the matter?" I ask. "Jealous because puberty hasn't come yet? Don't worry, Weaselwrench. Eventually, when you get your big-boy voice, you'll get some big-boy body parts to go with it."

"HA! You and your big-boy body parts!" he sneers. "I mean seriously . . . every news station in the city made such a big deal out of such a . . . small issue."

I feel a spark of anger, and for the barest instant, I forget my training. I just want to wipe that stupid sneer off his stupid face. I fire a sloppy right hook. He avoids it easily but doesn't take a shot. He knows he's gotten to me. "But then again, maybe you like the attention," he says, a twisted little smirk on his face. "Maybe you like everyone looking at your—"

"Shut up!" I say, and fling another sloppy right. This one he avoids completely. When I follow through, I'm completely off balance. He spins away from me, his back against mine for a moment, and then he grabs my right arm and flings me off the roof.

"See you later, Bright Buns!" he calls after me.

"Way to go, kid," I can practically hear Louis's voice in my head say as I fall. "Remember that lesson about not letting your enemy get under your skin and distract you? You know, the one I teach you JUST ABOUT EVERY DAY? Yeah, well, you just failed it. Now pull yourself together and act like a professional."

I fall ten stories, onto the roof of the shorter building next door. I'm not seriously hurt, but ten stories are ten stories; I'm going to be sore in the morning. I pick myself off the ground, leap over to the other building, and start climbing. I have to get back in the fight before they do Phantom some serious damage.

Sure enough, Dr. Chaotic has managed to pin Phantom Justice's arms behind his back in some sort of electrified netting. Monkeywrench is whaling away on Phantom's face and stomach. Phantom is taking the blows; he looks tired but unhurt for the most part. The news copter is catching all of this, which means that everyone watching at home knows that I'm a complete failure. I leap the length of the roof and tackle Monkeywrench.

"Get offa me, you perv!" he yells.

Without the distraction of Monkeywrench, Phantom Justice is able to break free from Chaotic's netting. I look behind me to see if Phantom needs a little help, just in time to see him rip an entire half-ton air-conditioning unit off the roof and hurl it at Dr. Chaotic. I guess he's OK. The air conditioner grazes Chaotic's armor, just enough to throw it out of whack. The armor is now sparking and twitching.

While I'm watching this, Monkeywrench is able to squirm out from under me. Rather than continue the fight, the little coward bolts, firing one last parting shot over his shoulder: "See you around, pervert!"

Dr. Chaotic also bolts, but neither Phantom nor I have anything left in the tank to give chase. It's hard enough just to stand. My shoulder and ankle are already starting to stiffen up. I limp over to Phantom Justice. "You OK?" I ask him.

"Yeah," he says. "It'll take more than what that little gnat has to hurt me."

I nod. I wish I could say the same thing.

5

AFTER MY LOUSY SHOWING AGAINST
Monkeywrench, I can't sleep. Every time I close my eyes, I see that little jerk's twisted smile as he looks down at my tights . . . I hear the screechy voice as he points and laughs. "Nice costume, Bright Buns! Ha-ha-ha-ha-ha!"

Trent is still asleep when I leave for school the next day. I can tell right from the start that it's going to be an awful day. Just picking up my backpack is an exercise in agony. I'm groggy from the lack of sleep, and everyone at school can't stop talking about what an idiot I am. I'm able to tune it out for most of the day, but after a while it really builds up. I'm on my way to seventh period when I start to lose my cool.

"Oh, man . . . Phantom Justice was getting POUNDED!" Some kid from my math class (I think his name is Justin) is talking to a small group of his friends from the lacrosse team. Justin (I think) is the son of some singer from some band I should probably know, but don't. "Where the heck was Bright Boy?" he yells.

"Changing his tights," one of the lacrosse kids says. Everybody laughs.

"Monkeywrench must've really messed him up," some other lacrosse kid says.

"He came back at the end," I hear myself say. The kids turn to look at me. I'm not sure if their confused expressions are because I'm defending Bright Boy, or because everyone in school knows that kids who aren't on the lacrosse team aren't supposed to talk to kids who are on the lacrosse team. It's an unwritten rule. "He knocked Monkeywrench off of Phantom."

"Yeah . . . nothing like coming in after it's almost over," Justin says. "Where was he before that? Phantom Justice needs a better sidekick. I bet I could do it." His friends loudly agree that he could.

Usually, I laugh stuff like this off . . . but it's been a tough week. "Uh, no you couldn't," I say. "You guys have ab-so-lutely no clue what it takes to be Phantom Justice's sidekick, OK?" Everyone is looking at me like I just grew an arm out of my forehead.

"Oh, like *you* do?" Justin says. And now he's up in my face, and it's taking all of my willpower not to fling him down the hallway on his head.

"I know better than you," I say before I can stop myself. Oh God . . . what am I doing?!

Everyone starts laughing. "Yeah, right!" Justin says. "Tell us what you 'know.'"

I'm tired, and not thinking straight, but I'm also frustrated. I'm this close to flipping around the hallway, leaping onto the ceiling, then yelling into all their faces, "I'm Bright Boy! I always have been! I've been right here under your noses!" I want them to see up close what I'm capable of . . . just how fast and strong I am, because they seem to have no idea how far out of their league I am. And then I want to explain to them that even though I'm a plus/plus, I still train my butt off. Why? The same reason they practice lacrosse, even though they already know how to play. The difference is that if Justin and his buddies fail, they lose a lacrosse game; if I fail, some nutjob takes over the world.

I'm this close to opening my big, fat mouth, when a hand closes onto my shoulder. The hand tries to whirl me around, but at the moment, I don't want to go, so I don't. I just stand there, stubborn and defiant. Then I notice all the lacrosse kids watching me, and I know that if I don't drop it, I'm going to have a lot of questions to answer . . . a lot of rumors to crush. The hand on my shoulder tightens its grip. I can barely feel it. I sigh, then start my act.

"Ow," I say with all the enthusiasm I can muster . . . which isn't much. "That really hurts." I turn around, and come face-to-face with Jake Berkshire and his group of idiots.

"Hello, Snot," he says, as if changing my name from Scott to Snot is still the funniest thing anyone has ever done ever. His friends laugh as if to confirm it . . . again. I sigh . . . again. I know the most painful thing about this encounter for me is going to be Jake's "jokes."

"Get outta here," he tells all the other kids. They all leave without a second thought. "What are you doin' in my hallway, Snot?"

There isn't a correct answer to that question, so I just keep my mouth shut. In a weird way, Jake and his friends just pulled me out of hole. They stepped in right as I was on the verge of giving my identity away. In a weird way, I'm grateful, and I'm not about to waste my second chance by losing my temper.

"I'm talkin' to you, Snot. I said what are you doin' in my hallway?"

"Yeah!" one of Jake's friends shouts. "Sissy!" another one says. The goodwill I felt for them is just about gone. I'm back to restraining myself from hurting them.

"I asked you a question, jerk-face!" Jake says, then punches me. It's a ridiculous punch, and I almost mistime my reaction because it takes forever to get to my jaw. I go limp and roll with it, so that Jake doesn't snap his wrist. It feels like someone just hit me in the face with a balled-up tissue. His friends start laughing and cheering, and I'm using all my willpower to not put them in the hospital.

Then Jimmy "Cracked Ribs" Douglas tells Andrew "Broken Arm" Buckley, Shane "Concussion" McConaughey, and Jake "Multiple Fractures" Berkshire that he thinks I've had enough. For his act of thoughtfulness, I mentally downgrade Jimmy to "bruised sternum."

Before the fight can go any further, lo and behold Dr. White, the foreign languages teacher, comes around the corner, just as she did yesterday. "Hey! Break it up!"

Jake and his friends stop in their tracks. They look nervous. This time, I'm trying not to laugh.

"Break what up, Dr. White?" Jake says, a look of cagey innocence on his face.

Dr. White levels an intense stare at him. Impressively, Jake never drops his eyes.

"Oh, this is not what it looks like. Scott here fell down, and my friends and I were just helping him up. Right, guys?" Jake's friends look like they're going to sprain something "yeah" and "of course"-ing to his suggestion.

Dr. White's eyes narrow behind her half-rim glasses. "Mr. Berkshire, there are some people in this school who are impressed with your charm. I am not one of them."

"Well let's just ask Scott what happened," Jake says. "See what he says."

"Well, Mr. Hutchinson?" Dr. White asks. "Are you going to stand up for yourself, or are you going to perpetuate Mr. Berkshire's awful bully cliché?"

I look over at Jake. He's desperately trying to give me a threatening look, and I burst out laughing. It's a reaction that no one expects, least of all me.

"Mr. Hutchinson?" Dr. White asks, a new note of concern in her voice, as if I had just gone crazy right before her eyes. Jake and his friends have an odd look on their faces. It takes me a minute to realize it's fear.

"I'm fine, Dr. White. It's just like they said. I'm a bit clumsy, and I fell. These guys were nice enough to help me up."

Jake's relief is clear on his face. For such a "bad boy," he has a real hang-up about getting in trouble. What a joke.

Dr. White knows we're lying, and we know Dr. White knows we're lying. I see a look on her face that I've seen on the faces of hundreds of criminals . . . a face that says, "How far do I really want to push this?"

"Get out of here," she says to Jake and his friends, even though she's clearly not happy about it.

"Yes, Dr. White," Jake says in a sacchariney voice. "See you around, Scott. Try to be more careful next time." The innocent grin never leaves his face.

"Come on, Mr. Hutchinson. I'll walk you to your class," she says when Jake and his friends are gone.

"That's not really necessary."

"That's not for you to determine."

"Oh."

She walks next to me the whole way. I try to act casual by looking at the paintings of old white men that line the walls, but it's not working. I'm very conscious of my movements. I feel awkward, knowing that she's watching me. She's an attractive woman, in a severe, intimidating way. Everything about her is precise. Her black suit almost looks like a military uniform; her hair is slicked down close to her skull and pulled into a tight bun. She's very sharp. I have to be careful. I don't want to give anything away.

"You shouldn't let them push you around like that," she says. "There are a lot of bullies in this world. You don't want to go through life doing whatever someone bigger says."

I burst out laughing again. I can't help it. There are times when the gap between my identities is so huge, it's ridiculous.

"Is something funny?" she asks.

"I laugh when I'm nervous," I say.

She stops walking and looks at me. I try to keep going, but it's just too weird, so I stop too. She stands there, staring at me. I start to get antsy. "What?" I ask.

She stares at me for a couple of more beats. "Nothing," she says, even though it was something. It was definitely something. "We're here."

I look up. It's the door to the class I was supposed to be in ten minutes ago. I open the door. "Mr. Hutchinson. Off doing a little independent study?" Mr. Privet, my social studies teacher, says.

I turn toward Dr. White, but she's already gone. Odd.

"Mr. Hutchinson?" Mr. Privet says. I turn back to him. The rest of the class giggles and whispers.

"Yes, sir," I say. I start fidgeting, playing with the big gold school crest on my sweater.

"Excellent! I expect a full report on your findings by the end of the day. Now, would you please take your seat?"

I bite my lip and take my seat without a word. I pass a kid with a picture of Bright Boy, cut out from the newspaper, on his desk. He's in the middle of drawing various parts of the male anatomy on it. I clench my hands into fists to prevent myself from grabbing the picture and making the kid eat it.

I plop myself down in my seat and try to concentrate on the lesson, but I can't. I feel so restless and wound up and frustrated; I feel like my molecules are going to fly apart at any moment. I just want to leap out the window and flip from building to building until I run out of buildings. Then I want to turn around and do it again.

Instead, I sit and watch my classmates as they take what they consider to be "risks." One girl passes the girl next to her a note. They both look at a kid (who I think is the captain of the baseball team) and start to giggle. The kid never notices them. A couple of other guys use some complex hand signals to communicate with each other from across the room. Another kid (I think his name is Sam) shows his friend (Max, maybe?) his raunchy picture of Bright Boy. They both snicker as quietly as they can, but Mr. Privet hears them and turns around.

"Let's keep the disruption to a minimum," he says in a tone that's stern, but not yet annoyed.

All the kids who were "breaking the rules" blush, but smile, as if they're both ashamed and exhilarated by almost getting caught. It's funny, because I never really break the classroom rules, not because I'm a "good guy," but because I don't have anyone to break them with.

Basically, I have no life (social or otherwise) as Scott, and now my hero identity isn't comfortable anymore either. I mean, becoming Bright Boy has always been my escape. Have a bad day as Scott? No problem! Just slap on the uni, go out, bust some skulls, and become a hero to millions. But now, that's completely changed. My stupid costume has made me joke. And I feel stuck . . .

I put my elbows on the desk and rest my head in my hands. I'm exhausted by it all.

"Are you OK?"

I lift my head up. Apparently, class ended. I must

have fallen asleep. Everyone else in the room is gone, except for me . . . and Olivia Duchamp, who is standing in front of me with a concerned look on her face. It takes me a moment to realize that her concern is for me.

"Sorry?" I ask.

"Are you OK? You look like you're not feeling well."

"I'm fine. I just . . . I'm just a little tired."

She's easily the prettiest girl I've ever talked to who wasn't falling off a building. Her friends Charlene and Allison are standing behind her. They look like they're not sure why Olivia is talking to me. I hope they don't look to me for an answer, because I don't have a clue.

"Are you sure?" she asks.

"Am I sure what?"

"Are you sure it's just being tired?" She starts to put her hand on my shoulder, but then stops, as if it might be a little too much to touch me the very first time we talk to each other.

"I think so," I say.

"Olivia," Allison says, stepping forward, "stop with the third degree. If he says he's tired, he must be tired. Come on."

"OK," Olivia says. "Sorry."

I shoot Allison a dirty look, even though I don't

really mean to. To tell you the truth, I'm actually a little relieved. I don't have any idea how to talk to a girl like Olivia. But just because I'm relieved doesn't mean I wanted it to end.

"Don't apologize," I say. "It was nice of you to ask."

Olivia gives me a warm smile that I can't help but return. "If you ever need anyone to talk to, Steve, just ask, OK?"

Steve. She thinks my name is Steve. And she's looking at me so warmly, I just don't have the heart to correct her. "You bet," I say. "Thanks."

She smiles and nods, then lets her friends drag her out of the room.

Steve?! Frickin' *Steve?!*

Suddenly, I want to hit someone . . . just punch someone dead in the face. And there's nothing I can do about it right now. I can't fight anyone in school, even Jake Berkshire; I'd kill them. Who can I hit?!

Monkeywrench. That's who. It takes very little effort on my part to make that little weasel the face of the misery my life has become, with his jokes about my outfit, and his stupid, squeaky laugh.

Monkeywrench.

My fingers start tingling at the thought of hitting

him, hard and often. He's a plus/plus. He can take it. I've got a lot of anger and frustration. It'll feel good to work some of it out on his face.

6

It's night, and Phantom Justice

is leaping from rooftop to rooftop a few paces in front of me. I hoped that becoming Bright Boy would help me feel a little less awkward after the day I had, but it's not really working. The only thing that's keeping me going is the fact that we're responding to an alarm, and Phantom is pretty sure that Dr. Chaotic tripped it . . . and wherever Chaotic is, Monkeywrench is, too. Apparently, they're at some warehouse stealing something. I don't know what; at the moment, I don't even care. The only thing I care about is whaling on Monkeywrench as soon as poss—

I run face-first into Phantom Justice's chest. Apparently, he had stopped in front of me and turned around without me seeing. "Is something wrong?" he whispers intensely.

"No . . . I—"

"You're not embracing the night."

"Uhh . . . what?"

"You seem a little preoccupied."

"Oh. Right . . . well, maybe a little."

"We've talked about this," he says. "You can't be out here if your head's not clear. The night will consume you."

"Right . . . no, I know . . . it's just . . . I have a lot going on right now."

"Like?"

"Nothing . . . it's . . ."

"OK, then let's just—"

"Everything sucks right now, OK?" I blurt out. "The only time I feel halfway normal is when I'm in this costume. And look at it. It's ridiculous."

"I don't—"

"It is. It's ridiculous! Kids at school call me a pervert. Not me . . . like Scott me . . . Bright Boy me. They think I'm a pervert!"

"The evil in this city festers like an open sore, and you're worried about some petty insults. Just ignore them."

"I try! But they're everywhere! The whole school is laughing at me! Even the kindergartners!"

"Those kids make fun of you because they're jealous. Most of them would trade places with you in a heartbeat."

"That's nice, but it doesn't make things any easier."

"So, is that why you do this? To be admired and loved?" he asks.

"No . . . But I don't do it to be constantly ridiculed, either."

He turns away from me. I can see his jaw tightening under his mask. "I need you to focus on the task at hand," he says, going back to his scary whisper. "Otherwise, you'll have to go home."

"Fine," I say. "I'll focus."

He looks at me and squints in his trademark "Don't lie to me because I can see the evil in your soul!" way, but I've seen it way too many times for it to be effective. Plus, if he could REALLY see the "evil in my soul," like what I was planning to do to Monkeywrench's face, he wouldn't have let me out of the house in the first place.

"Let's go," he snarls. And with a dramatic turn of his cape, he continues forward, toward the warehouse.

I roll my eyes and follow.

Three minutes later, we arrive at the industrial park

full of warehouses where we traced the alarm. Everything is quiet.

"Where are the police?" I ask.

"They're probably on their way. Do you want to wait for them," he asks with a mischievous grin, "or are you up for a little action?"

"You have to ask?" I respond. I only hope it's Dr. Chaotic and Monkeywrench. The thought of beating on someone other than them would be a total letdown.

We go through two warehouses; on the third, we hit pay dirt.

Dr. Chaotic and Monkeywrench are standing in front of a huge pile of crates, each one labeled with an IGO logo. We play the shadows and try to sneak up on them. Apparently, we're not as good at it as we think we are.

"You boys are late," Dr. Chaotic says as he turns to us. "We almost left without you. Ha-ha-ha-ha!"

"You're going back to prison, Chaotic," Phantom growls. "It's up to you whether you go in one piece . . . or several."

"Ooooh! Such tough talk! Is that to compensate for the fact that you run around with an adolescent boy in tights? Hm?"

My scalp starts to tingle, and I feel my face get hot.

"You see?" I whisper to Phantom. He makes a "take it easy" motion with his hand. No, he doesn't see.

"What are you up to, Chaotic?" Phantom asks.

"What, you think I'm just going to tell you? Huh? What fun would that be?"

"This is all a big game to you, isn't it?"

The two of them continue, back and forth, as if there's a big cliché contest and they're both determined to win. I've stopped listening. I can't stop staring at Monkeywrench. The voices of Dr. Chaotic and Phantom Justice become distant drones. The only things that exist in the world right now are Monkeywrench and my hatred for him . . . and he hasn't even noticed yet. He's watching the exchange between Chaotic and Phantom, because that's what we sidekicks usually do: We stand around and wait for the main event to start, and then we fight. I mean, that's why we're called sidekicks; if we were supposed to start the fighting, we'd probably be called *frontkicks* or something.

He seems fidgety . . . restless. He shoots me a couple of quick glances, but he doesn't really "see" me. He couldn't have . . . because if he did, he'd see the way I'm looking at him. He'd see the anger written all over my face.

He glances over at me again, but this time, something about me catches his eye. And so this time, he takes a

really long look . . . and he sees that I'm staring at him
. . . more like glaring at him . . . trying to break his legs
by sheer force of will. And he sees this. He sees how
angry I am at him . . . and he smiles. The little jerk
smiles! My teeth grind together. He smiles wider, and
then he blows me a kiss!

The next thing I hear is my own yell as I start
sprinting for Monkeywrench.

His eyes go wide. He wasn't expecting this. To be
fair, neither was I.

"What are you—ooof!" is all Monkey can get out
before I ram into him.

We break through the outside wall of the warehouse,
slamming into the side of a news van parked there. It
leaves a large, Monkeywrench-size dent in it. Reporters
scatter . . . some scream. Then they see the hole in the side
of the building, and realize that we're just the sidekicks,
and the main event is inside. They forget their fear and
rush past us, jockeying for position. I look through the
hole I just created, and for a moment, before the hole
is filled with press, I can see Phantom Justice and Dr.
Chaotic looking back at me. They look confused. I may
have jumped the gun a little.

"What is your problem?" Monkeywrench yells at me.
I turn my attention to him.

"You blew me a kiss. I wanted to return the favor."

"Return this," he says, and shoves his hand into my chin. I lift my right knee and catch him in the stomach, slamming the back of his head into the van again. I fall butt-first onto the ground. Before I have a chance to hit him again, he turns, leaps, flips, and lands on top of the van. Then he sprints off, leaping from van rooftop to van rooftop. He's heading for the nearest warehouse roof.

I sprint after him, staying to the ground. There's a van parked close to the warehouse where Monkey is heading. I leap on top of it, then leap from the van onto the warehouse roof. He's six feet away from me and sprinting for the next warehouse. "Stop!" I yell.

"No!" he yells, and keeps sprinting, but maybe he's a little rusty from his years away, or maybe I'm just faster than he is. I make up the ground between us and grab his arm. He tries to flip me, but I block him, flipping him instead. From the ground, he sweeps my legs out from under me. I fall hard on my back. He comes at me with an elbow, but I block and throw off. I flip up to a fighting position. He does the same. We're both breathing hard. The roof feels a little squishy under my feet, like all it's had to deal with are raindrops for the past thirty years . . . and we're a little bigger than raindrops.

"All right, perv . . . what else—"

"Shut up," I say. "Shut your freakin' mouth. You say one more word, and I swear you'll be trying to pick up your teeth with broken fingers."

"Ha! Next time you try to steal a tough-guy line from a movie, you might want to consider changing your tigh—"

I tackle him. We land on his back. The roof protests, making a loud, angry groan.

"Get off of me!"

"No time," I say.

"What?"

The roof gives way. I guesstimate that the fall is about thirty-five feet, because it hurts—a lot—but we're both still alive.

I roll over slowly, onto my knees and elbows. I take a few deep breaths. They hurt. I spit a couple of times. No blood. I wait to see if I go into shock. Nope. Just shaken up.

I can hear Monkeywrench wheezing beside me, and I don't feel so much like pummeling him anymore. Even if I wanted to, I'm not sure I could raise my arms. I get to my feet, slowly . . . I'm not sure my legs will hold me. "Are you OK?" I ask.

"No!" he says, and his voice sounds different . . . less screechy than normal.

"Don't try to get up," I say, and start to walk over to him.

"Stop!" he yells.

"I'm not going to hurt—"

"STOP!"

But I don't. I walk over to him. He's trying to pick himself off the ground as quickly as possible, but he's too shaken up.

I grab his arm to help him. "It's o—"

And that's when I notice Monkeywrench's mask is gone . . . and that Monkeywrench isn't a "he."

"Allison? Mendes?"

She screams, as if her real name is the filthiest insult I could ever call her. Suddenly, she's on me, all hands and elbows and nails. She's coming at me with a ferocity I've never seen. By the time I realize what she's up to, it's too late; she's already ripped my mask off.

I freeze. I put my hands up against my face, to try to cover it, but it's too late. She's already seen me.

"Uhh . . . you!" she shouts, then looks away.

My expression changes from fear to annoyance.

"You don't know who I am, do you?"

"Yes, I do. You go to my school."

"OK, great. So what's my name?"

She pauses, scrunches up her face, starts looking around the room, as if she's hoping that some friendly and helpful psychic might've predicted this moment and written my name on one of the walls.

"You don't know?! Seriously?" I shout.

"I'm sorry!" she says. "We must not have any classes together."

"We have five together!" I yell. "Five! And I sit right behind you in three of them!"

"Sorry! I said I'm sorry!"

"You and your friend Olivia came up and talked to me today! Today!"

She snaps her fingers. "Steve!" she says triumphantly.

"No!"

"Yes! Olivia called you Steve!"

"Yeah, she called me Steve, but that's not my name."

"Then why didn't you correct her?"

"Well . . . I . . . look . . ." I stammer. "Don't you think we have something a little more important to deal with right now?"

"Yeah . . . you're right," she says. She points at my tights. "You really need to cover up, Steve. It's obscene . . ."

"I get it! You can see my—! I'm wearing tights! I know! But you're not allowed to be mean to me until you figure out my real name."

"I'm not allowed to be mean to you? Aren't we like mortal enemies or something?" she asks.

"I don't know! Yes?"

"Why are you yelling?!"

"I DON"T KNOW! Wait . . . stop . . . just stop!" I say. "This is just . . . You're a girl from school."

"Yeah."

"You don't think this is weird?"

She shrugs. "Maybe if I knew your real name," she says, but there's a sly little smile on her face.

I smile back. I can't help it. This whole thing just got surreal.

"Of course, this is weird," she says. "Duh. The kid who sits behind me in pre-algebra is my archenemy."

"And whose name is . . ."

"Charlie?"

"Ugh. Charlie?"

"I don't know. Listen, the main battle is moving this way, so—"

"So, I'll just hold you here until Phantom Justice gets here. Then he and I will—stop laughing—he and I will—come on. Stop laughing."

"I can't help it," she says. "What makes you think I'm going to stick around?"

"You don't have a choice."

She laughs again, then starts scaling some boxes, heading for the hole in the roof we fell through.

"Wait!" I yell. "Where are you going?"

"Home."

"No, you're not. You were committing a crime. You're going to the police."

"No. *I* am going home to finish some homework, take a nice hot bath, and figure out how to keep you from freaking out at school tomorrow."

"Wha—you think you can just waltz out of here?"

"'Waltz out of here?' OK, Grandpa. Listen, here's the thing. You may have seen my face, but I've also seen yours. It's called 'mutually assured destruction.' As long as you don't tell who I am, I won't tell who you are. Got it?"

"Wait—!"

She drops my mask on the ground at my feet. "See you in school tomorrow, Bright Boy." She leaps out the hole in the ceiling. Just as I'm about to go after her, Dr. Chaotic and Phantom Justice crash through the wall.

I pick my mask up and slap it on my face. The sticky stuff has dirt on it, so it won't stay without me keeping a finger on each side.

Dr. Chaotic, using one of his jet-propelled boots, flies out the same hole that Allison . . . uh . . . Monkeywrench flew out. "So long, Phantom! See you around! HA-HA-HA-HA!"

"Are you all right, Bright Boy?" Phantom Justice asks.

"Yeah . . . Monkeywrench rabbited, though." I take my fingers off my mask, but it starts to fall off, so I quickly slap it back on.

"Is there something wrong with your mask?"

"Uhh . . ." Oh boy. My mind feels like its been wiped clean. I stand there with my mouth open, not sure how to even begin to explain. Before I have a chance to try, reporters start streaming into the warehouse.

"Come on," Phantom says, then leaps up the boxes and out the hole in the ceiling. I follow, still holding my mask in place.

7

"ARE YOU SURE YOU'RE OK?"

Phantom Trent keeps looking over at me as he drives. When he's acting like Trent but still dressed like Phantom Justice, I call him Phantom Trent . . . never to his face, only in my head.

"I'm fine."

"Do you want to talk about it?"

Do I want to talk about it. Do I want to talk about my complete and utter failure to protect the single most important aspect of my job—the one thing above all others that I need to keep secret, and not reveal to ANYONE, least of all the sidekick to our most dangerous enemy, because it turns every norm I've ever known into a possible "hostage-to-be-used-for-leverage"? Do I want to talk about how one of the prettiest and most intelligent girls in school is the sidekick to a criminal mastermind/sociopath, and yet still manages to be more popular than I am? Do I want to talk about how I'm actually a little excited by the fact that I'm probably going to see a lot more of Allison Mendes, even if this does lead to my death and the city's eventual destruction? Sure, I'll talk about it. Right after I figure out if I'm going insane or not, I'll talk about whatever you want.

"You know, you can't just go off half-cocked like that and start attacking people," Trent says.

"Huh?"

"You attacked Monkeywrench before the fight started. You're supposed to wait for your cue."

"Oh. Right. That."

"Yeah, 'that.' What else would I mean?"

I don't know . . . maybe our archenemies finding out our secret identities? "Nothing," I say.

"It was reckless," he says. "We hadn't had a chance to survey the scene. What if the warehouse was wired and one of them had a detonator?"

"You mean like that time you attacked Pocks?"

Phantom Trent shoots me an annoyed look.

Pocks was a plus/plus villain we faced off against

about four or five times. Now, we've gone against some serious mouth-breathers in our time, but Pocks made the dumbest of them look like Stephen Hawking. First of all, the name: Pocks. He intended it to be Pox, like "a pox on your firstborn" kinda thing. It's a horrible name, any way you slice it. I mean, who still uses the word *pox*? But then, he made things worse by spelling it P-o-c-k-s, because that's how he thought it was spelled. So that's what he had printed on his business cards. That's right. Business cards. He even stopped in the middle of one of our fights to hand me one. I still have it. It says, "Pocks—Agent of Mayhem! A Pocks on You!" He could have knocked me out right then and there, because I just kept staring at the card, not sure what to do. He didn't touch me, though. He said he liked that I really read it . . . that I let it all sink in. He didn't start fighting again until I had put the card in a safe place (he wanted to make sure I didn't lose it; they were kind of expensive to print).

So one day, about ten months ago, Pocks manages to score himself a boatload of explosives, which you know right from the start is not going to end well. He spends the whole night wiring up about half of the cars in a used car lot. Why a used car lot? We're still not sure. It's not exactly the first place a supervillain would think to hit, which is maybe why he picked it. He didn't seem to realize that the reason supervillains don't hold used car lots hostage is because . . . well, who cares? They're used cars. Even the guy who owns the lot wouldn't care all that much if everything blew up; he'd get most of his money back in insurance . . . plus all that free publicity.

So, Pocks has half the cars on the lot wired with explosives when we show up. Phantom starts in with one of his "opening confrontation" speeches. Meanwhile, Pocks keeps saying, "You're early. You're early" (as if we were supposed to wait for him to finish wiring all the cars before we confronted him). After a little bit of awkward silence, Pocks starts talking about how we can't stop him, and if we even try, he's going to hit the button on his detonator and blow up all these cars. The problem? He can't find the detonator. He starts searching all his pockets, but it's not in any of them. He starts sweating, and looks like he's going to apologize to us at any moment . . . but he's still saying his speech, which has lines in it like "You can't stop me!" and "I'll blow us all to pieces! I don't care!" And I'm trying not to laugh because the threats are obviously meaningless without the detonator, which he still can't find. To tell you the truth, I felt kinda bad for him.

So, Pocks is yelling these meaningless threats at us,

and the more he does, the more pissed off Phantom Justice looks. Finally, Phantom loses his cool and rushes him. Pocks looks really surprised, like he expected us to wait for him to find the detonator before we did anything . . . like he was following some script that Phantom and I were supposed to have but didn't. So . . . Phantom picks Pocks up and throws him about thirty yards; he lands on his butt on top of one of the wired cars.

Now Pocks had checked his back pockets at least a half dozen times while we were listening to his speech, but he hadn't found the detonator. It must've been in one of them, though, because literally half a second after landing on his butt—*KABOOM!* Half the lot exploded, taking Pocks along with it.

It took them a while, but the police eventually found all of Pock's pieces.

"Right . . . Pocks," Trent says, and even though the Pocks example proves his point, he seems annoyed that I brought it up. "You realize that we are all that's protecting the good people of this city from the clutches of evil."

"Right . . . clutches."

"What possible reason could you have had to justify breaking protocol?"

"I don't know," I say. "I guess I just snapped. Probably

something to do with yet another person making fun of my costume."

Phantom Trent sighs. "Back to the costume again. I thought we settled that."

"No, you settled that. I'm still the one who has to live with the ridicule."

"I thought we settled that, too."

"Look, everyone is making fun of me. The kids at school, newscasters, *the villains* . . . EVERYONE. I'm sick of it. Can we PLEASE talk about a new costume?"

"We'll see."

"That means no, doesn't it."

"No, it means we'll see. Keep pestering me about it and it'll mean no."

"Fine." I slump in my seat and cross my arms. My mask peels off my face and falls into my lap.

"What happened to your mask?" he asks. "Why isn't it sticking to your face?"

"I might've gotten some dirt on it."

"Well, you really ought to check those things before you go out. What if it had fallen off during the fight?"

I don't say anything. I turn to stare out the window, hoping Trent doesn't see my reflection in the glass. I was never good at keeping a poker face.

"It fell off during the fight, didn't it?" he says.

"Not exactly. She pulled it off."

"She?"

"Yeah. Turns out Monkeywrench is a girl."

Trent slams on the brakes and pulls the car over. "What happened back there?"

"Can we talk about this later? We're kind of conspicuous out here—"

"Tell me what happened."

I take a deep breath, then let it out slowly. "We were fighting on top of one of the warehouses and the roof gave way. We fell like forty feet. I'm OK, really . . . thanks for the concern." He doesn't say anything, so I continue. "When I got up to check on Monkeywrench, I saw that her mask had come off."

"What happened to yours?"

"Well, after I saw her, she flipped out and attacked me. I thought she was trying to kill me. She wasn't. She was just trying to—"

"Get to your mask," he finishes.

"Yeah. 'Mutual assured destruction,' she said. I tell people who she is, she'll tell people who I am."

"She's smart. I'd expect nothing less from our main adversary."

"Right."

"So the girl is someone you know?" he asks.

"Yeah, I go to school with her. She's in my grade. I have a few classes with her."

"Hm."

He turns the wheel and hits the gas. We take off again.

"You don't seem that upset," I say.

"Being upset about it is a waste of energy. Instead, we need to figure out where to go from here."

There's a long pause.

"Soooo, what do I do?" I ask.

"*You* shouldn't do anything. As long as you don't tell, she won't tell, either. She can't."

"But what if she does?"

"Well, then we'll have to do something drastic, won't we?" There's an odd tone to his voice, almost as if he's smiling when he says it.

"What do you mean?"

"Nothing. Listen, this could actually be a good thing. We might able to use this to put an end to Dr. Chaotic's reign of terror once and for all."

"Really?"

"Yes. You two have to stay close to each other now, if for no other reason than to make sure that the other one isn't plotting something."

"OK . . . uhh . . . So, I'm supposed to go to school tomorrow and pretend like nothing happened?"

"No. You're going to pretend that you didn't tell me or anyone else anything about this," he says. "You're going to get to know her. You're going to get close to her . . . become friends with her. She's going to get comfortable with you . . . then one day she's going to slip up . . . get a little *too* comfortable, and accidentally reveal some important piece of information . . . and . . . Wham! That's when we've got them."

"OK, I guess. But . . . um . . . you know I'm not exactly great at making friends."

"I know. Louis has expressed some concern."

"Yeah, so . . . what if I just turn her in?"

"And let her give up your identity?"

I nod. "It would end their reign of terror, wouldn't it?" I say. I don't tell him that at the moment, I don't think giving up my identity would be that big a loss.

"Yes, except that you wouldn't just be giving up your own identity; you'd also be giving up mine, and who else would keep darkness from engulfing the city?"

"Yeah, but . . . couldn't we figure something out? Maybe get new identities or something?"

Trent turns to me. "You don't get it, do you? Once your identity is compromised, it'll be leaked to every news source in the world. Pretty soon your name and face will be beamed across the globe. Everyone will know who you are, what you look like, who your friends and relatives are, what you ate for lunch in the fourth grade, for heaven's sake.

"Not to mention, every criminal will know who you are," he continues. "And those vermin will do whatever they can to hurt you, or gain leverage against you. And the best way for them to do that would be to threaten your loved ones, from the past and the present . . . the people in your personal life who can't defend themselves against the power of evil."

"No, I know."

"Are you willing to put a bull's-eye on every person you know?"

"No, of course not," I say.

"Then you need to do your job and get over your shyness, or whatever it is. You need to do what is necessary."

"I didn't say I wasn't going to try," I say. "I'm just not sure I can succeed. I don't even know where to start."

"Don't make the first move. If you go to her, she may

feel like you're coming after her. Let her come to you. And when she does, just play it cool."

I almost laugh. Play it cool? Don't you have to be cool to play it cool? Does Trent even know me?

"Pretend like the whole bad-guy/good-guy thing is just a game to you," he says. "That you don't really do it out of any moral obligation or sense of justice. You're in it for the thrills."

"Right . . . OK . . . thrills . . ."

"You can do this, Scott. Just remember, there are lives at stake."

I try to give Trent a confident smile, but it comes out more like a grimace.

"All right," he says. "Good soldier."

I spend the rest of the ride home staring out the window. For the first time since I was a little kid, I find myself wishing for a completely different life.

8

"WHAT'S THE MATTER, KID?" LOUIS
says from the driver's seat.

"Mm," I respond. I'm exhausted and not up for conversation. Every time I closed my eyes to sleep last night, I kept having the same nightmare: I'm trying to drive a car on a windy mountain road, but I can't see anything because the windshield is blacked out. I try to stop, but the brakes don't seem to work. So all I can do is steer blindly and hope not to hit anything.

"Does it have something to do with you giving up your identity to your archenemy, and endangering everything and everyone in your life?" Louis asks.

"It's either that or that science test I didn't study for."

Louis laughs. "Well, at least you got a sense of humor about it."

"Yeah, it's great. I'm sure it's good to know that if some villain kills you, I'll be able to give a funny speech at your funeral."

"Gettin a little melodramatic there, don't you think?"

"OK, now I do. When the king of melodrama tells you you're being melodramatic, you tend to make a note of it."

Louis smiles. "Try not to let it get to you, kid. Things got a way of working out."

"Yeah, but what if my entire life becomes a disaster?" I ask.

"Well, technically, it would be worked out . . . just not in the way you hoped."

"Ugh. You're really lousy at making me feel better, you know that?"

"Thanks. Lemme ask you this: When's the last time you felt good? I mean really, really good?"

I stop and think about it. "I don't know."

"Don't you think that's a problem?"

"I don't know. Lots of people aren't happy all the time."

"Yeah," he says, "but how many people are never happy?"

I grimaced. "I wouldn't say I'm *never* happy."

"You're never happy. There. I said it for you."

"Thanks a ton. So you think blowing up my whole life is going to make me happier? Seriously?"

"Not necessarily," Louis says. "I'm just not sure it'll make you less happy than you already are."

"Well, that's depressing."

"Come on, kid . . . just between you and me, how do you feel about going to school today? About seeing her?"

"Freaked out."

"Honestly?"

"Yes and no . . . I'm excited, OK? Is that what you want to hear?"

"Yeah. That's exactly what I wanted to hear."

"Don't you think that's bizarre?" I ask. "This whole thing has the possibility to ruin my whole life, and I'm excited."

"Our feelings don't always make sense. They're not supposed to."

"It would be a heck of a lot easier if they did."

"Yeah, I guess so," Louis says, "but it would also make life a heck of a lot less interesting."

"Oh man . . . I didn't think you were going to turn this into a life lesson."

"Yeah well, if you didn't screw up, I wouldn'ta had to," he said with a wry smile on his face.

"You know, I'm not as upset about putting your life in danger anymore."

"The only thing that surprises me, kid, is that it took you this long."

"Ouch . . . OK, I surrender," I say. "So what do I say to her? Sorry for knocking you through a wall just doesn't sound right, especially since I'm not really sorry."

"Well, in my opinion, I think you gotta wait to see what she says first. Let her start the conversation; that way you got something to respond to. Don't think about it so much. See what she says first."

"So let her come to me. That's exactly what Trent said."

"He's right. You're already overthinking things. Any attempt to approach her on your part is going to feel forced, by her and you. Sincerity is your friend in this situation."

"Even if I'm lying?"

"Especially if you're lying."

Louis pulls the car in front of the school, and I have a weird rush of adrenaline, one that feels out of place when I'm in my Scott identity.

"Wish me luck," I say.

"Good luck, kid. Try to put up a better fight with her than you did with me."

"Had to get one last shot in, didn't you?"

Louis looks back at me and winks. "I'm from Brooklyn. 'One Last Shot' is our motto."

I get out of the car. As I watch Louis drive away, I'm full of the weirdest mixture of feelings: dread, hope, excitement, anger, fear. Half of me can't wait to get inside the school; the other half wants to run away, screaming.

The welcome chime rings. I take a deep breath, then walk up the stairs and into school.

When I get inside, it seems like just a normal day. Kids are all over the place, talking, laughing; some trying to gather their stuff quickly and get to class, others trying to milk every last second of hanging out in the hallway. I feel like I have a big sign on my back that says I'm Bright Boy! But as I walk to my locker, it starts to sink in that there's still only two people who can see it: me and Allison.

I'm trying to figure out what to say to her if I happen to run into her in the hallway. I run through my options: fake laugh and a cool "Hey"; fake laugh and a "Crazy night last night, huh?"; fake laugh and a "What's shakin', bacon?" Ugh . . . those all suck. Should I drop the fake laugh? But how else can I appear like I'm cool and unaffected? Maybe, a finger snap? Or a double finger snap? Man, I am *not* good at this. Maybe I'll just let her kick me in the face . . .

When I get to my locker without seeing her, I'm a

little disappointed, but mostly relieved. I go through my normal morning routine, but it takes me a little longer since I stop every forty-five seconds to scan the hallway around me.

I'm a muttering-to-myself mess by the time I get to first period. Allison, on the other hand, strolls into the room as if she just had the best night of sleep in her life. She's giggling and chattering away with Olivia and Charlene. Olivia sees me looking at them and gives me a big smile. "Hi, Steve," she says. Charlene giggles. Allison smiles but doesn't look at me, even when she takes her seat . . . in the desk directly in front of mine.

She sits through the whole class without turning back once. Twice Mr. Privet calls on me, and twice I just stare at him blankly. The only thing I can concentrate on is the back of Allison's head. Meanwhile, she's answering questions like she's a winning contestant on a game show.

When the bell rings, she gets up and heads for the door, again without looking back. Olivia and Charlene wait for her. They all leave together and resume their chattering and giggling.

"Unimpressive performance today, Mr. Hutchinson," Mr. Privet says as I'm leaving. "Let's get it together, OK?"

Allison doesn't look at me once, all day. Not in the

three classes we have together in the morning. Not at lunch. Not in the two classes we have after lunch. Not a glance, or a wink, or double snap and a "What's shakin', bacon?" Nothing.

I'm starting to get antsy. Trent and Louis aren't always right about everything. The day's almost over. I've got to go up to her. I have to talk to her. I can't go through a whole night like this. What is her problem? How can this not be bothering her? I stand up to go talk to her. Unfortunately, I'm in the middle of Dr. White's Spanish class.

"Mr. Hutchinson? May I help you?"

The class giggles. Allison doesn't even turn around.

"No, Dr. White . . . just adjusting my pants."

This gets a laugh from the class.

"Thank you for sharing, Mr. Hutchinson, but can you please adjust your pants on your own time?"

"Yes, Dr. White."

"That means you should sit down now."

The class laughs again. I sit down. Well, that went well.

Allison sits closer to the door, so when class finishes, she's one of the first ones out. I hurry to catch up to her.

"Mr. Hutchinson." It's Dr. White.

I stop. The rest of the kids stream past me as I walk back into the classroom. "Yes, Dr. White."

"Something troubling you?" She's looking at me over the top of her half-rim glasses.

"No, Dr. White. My . . . uhh . . . pants were riding up a bit . . . you know how that goes," I say, then immediately have the urge to slap myself in the forehead. Did I really just try to start a conversation about wedgies with Dr. White? What is my problem? And what is with my sudden obsession with pants?

She sits there and looks at me without saying anything. "Is there something else that you wanted to talk to me about?" I ask.

"Possibly," she says. "But not yet. Good day, Mr. Hutchinson. Try to keep your pants on straight." She starts correcting the tests on her desk, as if I'm no longer there. I walk out of her room, feeling like I'm on shaky ground. I feel like I have that I'm Bright Boy! sign on again, only this time I'm not sure that only Allison and I can see it.

When I get out into the hallway, Allison is long gone. I have to find her. I'm through waiting for her to make the first move. I'm—

Someone grabs me by the back of the shirt and yanks.

I'm pulled backward into a dark room. The door slams. I throw a punch, more out of instinct than fear. The light clicks on.

"Whoa!" Allison says, and ducks my punch. "Watch it!"

I go on guard, waiting for a retaliatory punch, but she doesn't throw one.

"Put your guard down, hot shot," she says. "If I wanted to beat you up, I wouldn't drag you into a closet to do it."

"What do you want?" I ask.

"I want to stop you before you do something stupid, like cause a scene."

"Cause a scene? Why would I cause a scene?"

"I don't know. Then again, why would you repeat the phrase 'cause a scene' twice in two sentences? Maybe because you were thinking about—oh, I don't know—causing a scene?"

"No, I wasn't!" I shout.

"You're causing a scene right now, Bright Buns."

"Stop calling me Bright Buns, or I'll start calling you Monkey Face."

She looks at me for a second. "Well, well, well . . . look who has a snarky side. Deal. So you've finally gotten my attention. What do you want?"

"Oh, come on . . . this doesn't bother you?" I ask.

"What, standing in a closet? I've been in worse places."

"No . . . this! Us! We're archenemies!"

"Yeah. I know," she says. "Try to keep it down, would you?"

"That doesn't freak you out?"

"Yeah. It freaks me out plenty. I'm just a lot better at hiding it. Which isn't exactly a challenge. Man, you're high-strung! No wonder you don't have any friends."

"No," I say. "I don't have any friends because I spend most of my time putting people like you in jail."

"Ugh. Well, at least you answered the question: If a hero faces a villain and there's no one there to hear, does he still make a speech?"

"You're the one who pulled me in here . . . what do *you* want?"

"I want you to calm down so you don't blow this for the both of us."

"Fine. I'm calm."

"You don't sound calm."

"I'm not!" I yell. "I just don't get it . . . I mean this is bizarre, OK? You're like the biggest goody-goody in school, and it's all an act?"

"Well, kinda," she says. "I mean, I think I'm a good person."

"You're a sidekick to a sociopath!"

"My dad is not a sociopath."

"OK, then, what would you call him?"

"Hmm . . . focused. Unconventional. Not a great dancer."

"You don't have to do this," I say.

"Do what?" she asks in a peevish tone.

"Be a criminal. I can help you."

She starts laughing. "Help me? Help ME?! HA! You're the one exposing yourself every time you go out. Seriously, you're traumatizing half the city."

"All right . . . I get it . . . I wear tight pants. You've driven that point firmly into the ground. Now stop avoiding the question."

"You didn't ask me a question."

"I thought it was implied. How can you be Dr. Chaotic's sidekick? I know he's your father, but he's a villain!"

"Define 'villain,'" she says.

"Wha—? Villain! Someone who steals stuff, hurts people . . . you know, someone evil."

"Define evil."

"Oh, come on," I say. "Stop avoiding the question."

"I'm not," she says. "You're avoiding the answers."

"What?"

She sighs and rolls her eyes. "Come with me." She opens the door, grabs my wrist, and pulls me down the hall.

She drags me to the science lab that we're supposed to be in at the moment. Mr. Jacobs sees me first and looks annoyed, but when he spies Allison, his expression softens. "Allison . . . I'm sure you have a good explanation for being late." He says it not as a challenge, but as if he already knows it's true.

"Yes, I just saw the most interesting bees' nest outside, and since you're a big believer in independent study, and since we have a big project due in a couple of weeks . . ."

"You were wondering if you could skip class to study and observe it."

"Only if you think it's OK."

"Why do you need . . . ?"

"Scott," I say when his pause stretches a little too long.

"Scott," he repeats.

"I was thinking that he and I could partner up. He's a HUGE bee freak."

Allison hits me with an elbow, too fast for the naked eye to catch. "I like bees," I say. It comes out so stiff and awkward that Allison looks at me and almost cracks up.

"Well, bees' nests are fascinating. And I do applaud your initiative . . ." He thinks about it for a moment, then says. "Go ahead. But be careful! And I expect a full report on this."

"Thank you, Mr. Jacobs!" She grabs my hand and drags me off. I manage to get a quick look at the class before we leave. There are more than a few envious male faces.

"How did you do that?" I ask.

"Just have to lay the groundwork," she says. "I've spent years being a Goody Two-shoes. Years. So now, when I want to do something, I ALWAYS get the benefit of the doubt. Once you have that good girl label, you're set."

"Oh."

"Plus, all these teachers believe in unconventional teaching methods, otherwise they wouldn't be here; they'd teach at public school."

We head out the front door. I stop at the bottom of the stairs, not sure where to go next. Allison keeps walking. "Shouldn't we stay close to the building?" I ask.

She stops and turns to me. "How fast can you get back here if you needed to?"

"As Scott or—" I look around, then whisper, "*Bright Boy?*"

Allison looks amused. "There's no difference, dummy."

"Yeah, there is. I don't use my—*powers*—when I'm out of—*costume.*"

"OK, first of all, stop whispering. And second of all, we've been going to school together for how long? Did you ever see me use my powers?"

"No, but that's because you never—"

She's smiling at me.

"You use your powers all the time, don't you?"

"ALL the time. My God, I'm zipping around these halls like fifty times a day."

"How come I never saw you?"

She shrugs. "Maybe you're just not that observant."

I try to laugh her comment off, but it seems that there's more than a little truth to it.

"Come on," she says, and grabs my wrist again.

"Where are you taking me?"

"I'm not *taking* you anywhere. You're a big boy with super-strength. If you don't want to go, no one's going to force you." She lets go of my wrist and starts walking.

I catch up to her, walking in stride. I think about taking her hand, but I don't. She sees me looking at her hand, and she smiles. I smile back at her. "Try to keep up," she says, and sprints ahead of me.

I sprint after her. I'm breaking one of my rules . . . and it feels amazing. She looks back at me to see if I'm still behind her; she smiles when she sees that I am.

This is only a job . . . this is only a job . . . this is only a job . . .

9

DR. EDWARD SIMMONS IS IN HIS LAB.

a mile underground, trying to correct the trigger mechanism to his latest deadly invention. The pull is still too light, making it too easy to fire off an accidental shot . . . and you don't get to be Dr. Chaotic, Phantom Justice's most dangerous enemy, by firing off accidental shots. He starts to dismantle the trigger mechanism when the screwdriver slips from his hands. He snaps it out of the air quickly and with little fuss.

"I believe you were about to say 'Nice catch,' yes?" Edward says to what appears to be an empty room.

There's a pause, then a voice comes from one of the darkened corners. "It was a nice catch."

"How many times must I tell you that sneaking up on me is not possible?" Edward says. "The thrill you got from trying . . . it gave me a little tickle, right here." He points to a spot on his head, directly behind his right ear.

"Well, at least I circumvented your alarms."

"I turned them off. I had a feeling you were coming."

"Oh."

Edward quickly turns and pulls the trigger on the weapon he's holding, aiming it at the spot where the voice came from. The air is suddenly full of laser sound and ozone smell. Several large crates go flying, as if an invisible giant swatted them away.

"Still too light," he says, putting the weapon back on the table. He picks up his screwdriver again and starts tinkering.

"What the hell was that?" the voice asks, now from a different shadowy corner of the room.

"Weapons testing. And please stop the dramatics. I'm guessing you avoided that blast by about ten feet."

"Twelve."

"My mistake. Now . . . how about coming over here and taking a seat? I have no interest in speaking to the room for the next forty minutes," Edward says.

"Fine." Trent Clancy steps out of the shadows and laughs. "You're always so cranky when you can't get a trigger right."

"They're always the hardest part," Edward says. "I can build a damn laser that knocks over two-ton boxes, but I still have trouble making a simple trigger."

"You always figure it out." Trent sits on the arm of the worn leather armchair that's positioned like an afterthought in the middle of the room; he has a metal briefcase in his hand and a big grin on his face. "God, it's good to be working with a professional again! It's been strictly amateur hour around here since you took a break."

"Yes, so I've been reading. Not a whole lot of staying power to the new guys."

"Yeah. They have the speed and strength, but, man, are they dumb! They usually only last a couple of jobs before they quit."

"Or get fired," Edward says, and now he and Trent are staring at each other.

Trent is still grinning, but his eyes are cautious, watchful. "Accidents happen. Things . . . explode sometimes," Trent says in his Phantom Justice whisper-growl. "That's the risk you run when you deal with people who don't know what they're doing."

"Mm-hm." The two men stare at each other, their expressions inscrutable. "You know," Edward says, "I got that chair specifically for you to sit in, not on."

Trent laughs, and the moment is gone. "Whoa . . . Looks like you've got a case of the COMS today, Doc."

"What is—wait . . . COMS . . . Cranky Old Man Syndrome."

"Good guess."

"I never 'guess,'" Edward says. "Now, to what do I owe the pleasure of this midafternoon visit?"

"I come bearing gifts," Trent says, holding up the metal briefcase. He walks over to Edward, puts it on the table and clicks it open. It's full of neat stacks of hundred-dollar bills. "First installment. Do you want to count it?"

Edward smiles. "No need."

Trent smiles back. "Nice to know that we're still on the same page after all these years."

"It's an easy page to be on. "

"This is the first of seven," Trent says, tapping the top of the briefcase. "IGO thought smaller chunks would be easier to hide."

"Makes sense." Edward looks at the money in the briefcase.

"Man, it's good to be making some real money again! The amateurs were really putting a ding in the numbers," Trent says. "I'll tell you, Edward, if you said no to this, I think I would've had to turn them down. No way any of the other clowns had enough juice to pull off the kind of numbers IGO's talking about."

"Well, I guess you're lucky that private school is so expensive."

Trent looks at the weapon Edward is working on. "That for our next gig?" he asks.

"If I can get the damn trigger right."

Edward hands Trent the gun. Trent aims at the same crates that Edward knocked over before and pulls the trigger. They go flying across the room.

"Battering force," Edward tells him. "Same concept as the Pulverizer, but with none of that nasty laser burn. It may sting a little, but nothing too bad."

"Trigger felt fine to me," Trent says, handing the gun back to Edward. "Oh, and feel free to bring back the Pulverizer and use it on Bright Boy, if you want. That little pest could use some laser burn."

"Problems at home?"

"Ugh! What a little crybaby!" Trent groans, then runs his fingers through his hair. "'*Oh, my pants are too tight! Oh, people are making fun of me! Boo-hoo-hoo,*'" Trent says in a whiny voice.

"To be fair, his costume is a bit embarrassing."

"The hell it is! It's an icon!"

"All right . . . calm down."

"Maybe the problem is that he's just too old to wear it. Might be time to bring in someone younger, which would help boost the numbers in the youth demographic." Trent laughs, but it has a tight, cold sound to it. "Nothing like a sidekick death to boost the ol' numbers, right?"

"I didn't realize you hated him that much."

"Yeah, well, some days he can really push my buttons. You must feel the same way about . . ." Trent pauses.

"Allison."

"Yeah . . . Allison."

"Not really. She does her thing; I do mine. We try to stay out of each other's hair," Edward says without taking his eyes off his work.

Trent watches Edward intently for a moment, then looks around the room. He picks up some papers, looks at them without really seeing them, then puts them back down.

"Something else is on your mind," Edward says without looking up.

"Maybe."

"It wasn't a question. There *is* something else on your mind, and you're trying to decide whether to tell me or not. It feels like this"—Edward taps the top of his head with one finger—"so . . . please . . . save me the headache."

"Fine. The kids know about each other."

Edward stops working. He puts his screwdriver down. "What do they know?"

"Each other's secret identities."

"Hm. So that's what she was hiding from me this morning," Edward says. "Is that it?"

"As far as I know, yeah."

"What do you want to do about it?"

"Well, I'd love to leave Bright Boy bleeding in an alley somewhere," Trent says, a malicious grin on his face, "but I suppose I can wait."

"Hm. Wearing your hostility for him a little close to the surface these days, don't you think?"

"He's insufferable. Sometimes, he just makes me want to . . . gahhh!!" Trent yells as he punches one of the nearby crates. His fist goes right through.

Edward sighs. "As stable as ever, I see. How did you find out about them?"

"Scott told me everything. Last night, he and Allison were fighting, and they ended up falling through a warehouse roof," Trent says. "She lost her mask in the fall, then ripped Scott's mask off after he saw who she was."

"Yes, well, it was bound to happen."

Trent shrugs. "I'll tell you, though, it's a good thing your daughter's as mature as she is. I thought Scott was going to wet himself."

"Why? What did she do?"

"She told him flat out that if he tells on her, she'll tell on him. So . . . now they have this agreement based on mutual distrust." Trent laughs. "You know what Scott wanted to do?"

"Turn her in and throw his identity away in the name of justice."

"Yeah, do you believe it?"

"Yes. I've met the boy, remember? His constant barrage of 'heroic' thoughts feels like someone's giving me a noogie. You weren't planning on telling him about us, were you?"

"God, no! Can you imagine? He'd turn us in."

"He's a true hero, Trent. You should be proud." Edward keeps a straight face for a minute but then breaks out laughing.

Trent laughs with him. "Oh, I am. Wait 'til you hear the speech I wrote for his funeral."

Edward goes back to tinkering with the trigger on his weapon.

"So," Trent says, eyes fixed on Edward, "did you tell Allison . . . you know . . . about this?"

"No."

"Are you sure?"

Edward stops what he's doing and looks at Trent. "What is that supposed to mean?"

"That, Edward, is supposed to mean that I need to know exactly what's going on with us at all times. I have to be more cautious than you, considering I have a hell of a lot more to lose in this. You get caught, you just take another vacation. I get caught, and my whole life is in the toilet. So this may ruffle your feathers a bit, but I don't care. Now, do you think Allison knows?"

"No."

"Because if she finds out, she may get angry enough to tell Scott . . . and then we have a real problem."

"Would we?"

Trent smiles. "Well, I wouldn't have a problem. Scott would have a problem. And you."

"Me?"

"Let's just say that I'm not so sure anymore that if push comes to shove, you'll do what's necessary."

"And what makes you 'not so sure'?"

"Just an old-fashioned gut feeling. Not exactly plus intelligence, but it's always worked for me."

"Then maybe you should let me go. Cut your losses. Find someone else to take my place. Didn't you work with Rogue Warrior last week? Why don't you see if he's available?" Edward says. They stare at each other.

Trent's face relaxes a little. "Now, let's not get crazy. I'm just saying that Allison seems like a keeper, a lot better than my lousy sidekick. If I were you, I'd have a hard time parting with her. Just the thought of training someone else when you've already got a good one . . . ugh! What a headache!"

Edward doesn't say anything.

"It's just, well, I know that plus intelligences get smarter as they get older," Trent says, "but I've also heard that they get colder . . . more analytical . . . less emotional."

Edward gives a small nod.

"Well, if Allison isn't just another carbon life-form to you already, then she pretty soon will be. So you may have to decide which one of us makes more sense to have in your life after the love is gone, as they say. Her or me."

"Fine. Is that all?"

"I still haven't heard your answer."

Edward's jaw stiffens. "You know it's you."

"Do I?"

"Yes. And if you didn't, you do now."

They stare at each other for a few more seconds before Trent smiles. "Thank you, Edward. I mean . . . let's not get too intense! We're nowhere near that point . . . yet. But it's nice to know that I can still rely on you."

"Yes. Of course."

Trent picks up the weapon that Edward's been working on. He pulls the trigger, sending the crates from before crashing into the far wall of the lab. They splinter into a million pieces. "You're right, as usual. The trigger is much more precise now. So . . . are we doing this tonight?"

"No, we're not ready yet," Edward says. "I need to work on our plans. Our escapes have been getting a little sloppy lately."

"I don't think anyone notices but you."

"Yes, well, let's keep it that way. The last thing we need is an investigation."

Trent starts laughing. "Come on, Edward. Who's going to investigate us?"

10

"OH MY GOD, WHAT ARE THESE CALLED

again?" I ask. We're sitting on the ledge of a building, forty stories above street level, and I'm trying to shove an entire pita-meat-sauce thing in my mouth. It's the most amazing thing I've ever tasted.

"It's a gyro," Allison says, looking at me with a mixture of amusement and horror. "I can't believe you've never had one. I mean, this city has so many amazing things in it. Don't you just walk around sometimes? Check stuff out?"

"No," I say, but since my mouth is stuffed with gyro, it comes out like "fffo."

"Ugh," she says laughing. "Swallow before you talk, you frickin' barbarian. Jeez . . ."

"I am not a barbarian!" I say, spraying food all over the place.

She laughs and covers her face with her hands. "Gah! Stop!"

"Are you going to finish—?"

"Here," she says, handing me the rest of hers. "Aren't you afraid you're going to catch some 'villain-cooties'?"

"I'll take my chances," I say as I take an enormous bite out of the half-eaten gyro. "How could you not finish this?"

She shrugs. "I have them all the time." She smiles and cocks one eyebrow at me. "So . . . seriously . . . you never just walk around the city and get lost sometimes?"

I shake my head. "I only come into the city to go to school or go out on patrol."

"Well, now you know what you're missing."

I nod enthusiastically. Both gyros are gone, so I start licking the foil. I can't help myself. When I'm convinced that I've gotten every last drop of food and sauce, I ball up the wrappers. "I have to go," I say, and start to stand up.

"Why? We just got up here."

"I know . . . I just have to check in with Phantom. Things are kind of crazy right now, and I want to make sure he doesn't need me for anything."

Allison starts laughing.

"What?" I ask.

"If I'm here, chances are he doesn't need you."

"Oh . . . right . . ." I sit back down. "Well, aren't you worried that Dr. Chaotic might need you . . . for whatever you guys might be doing?"

"Nah. You guys are on call. We just follow a schedule," she says. She stands up and starts absentmindedly walking along the ledge, pointing her toes out on every step, like a ballerina. I notice, not for the first time, how long her legs are. I'm trying not to stare. "I think we should play a game."

"What kind of game?" My body tenses.

"Relax. Nothing to do with the whole cops and robbers thing . . . we already play that game enough, thank you very much. No, I think we need to play a game called One Question Each, and You Have to Answer Truthfully, or I'll Tell the World Your Secret Identity."

"Think of that on the spot, did you?"

She smiles. It's similar to one of the hundreds of smart-aleck smirks she gave me as Monkeywrench, but this one is softer and doesn't make me want to punch her in the face.

"I'll go first," she says. "Are you ready?"

"Fine, as long as it isn't a question about my costume."

"Why do you wear such a horrible costume?"

I sigh. My head drops.

"I mean, it's horrible," she continues. "You know that, right?"

"Yes."

"Well, thank God for that. I mean, it's top-to-bottom awful. Forget for a minute the fact that you are a borderline case of indecent exposure—God knows, I'm trying—no offense . . ."

"None taken," I say sarcastically.

"Seriously though, bright yellow tights and a red cape? Wow. The image of your outfit is literally burned onto my retinas."

"Do you have a question or not?"

"Yeah. Why do you wear it? It looks ridiculous, you clearly don't like to wear it. So why bother?"

"Because."

She pauses to see if there's more. There isn't.

"Because?" she says. "No, no, no. 'Because' is an answer that adults give to five-year-olds when they want them to shut up. Look at me? Do I look five?"

"No."

"No. So . . . answer my question or lose the game.

I swear to God I'll tell Lord Fauntleroy here your secret identity." She drapes her arms over the gargoyle and gives him a small kiss on one of his pointy ears.

"Lord Fauntleroy?"

"He's an aristocrat. Now answer!"

"I wear it because I have to."

"Says who? Phantom Justice?"

"Well, yeah," I say.

"Where are your parents?"

"Dead. Killed when I was four."

"Oh. Sorry. My mom's dead, too, if it makes you feel any better."

"Why would that make me feel better?" I ask.

"Yeah, I guess it doesn't work like that." She pauses. She looks at the ground for a second, then looks at me. "Do you remember them?"

"Bits and pieces," I say, and before I can stop it, an old movie of my parents starts playing in my head. They're helping me ride my bike in the driveway of a house I barely remember. My mom is helping me balance, even though it's obvious that I don't need any help. My dad is sitting in a lawn chair, making funny noises so I'll laugh until I fall over. My mom is getting annoyed with him, but not really. Mostly, he's making both of us laugh.

It was hard for her to get mad at him. It was hard for anyone to get mad at him.

"They were killed in a car accident," I continue. "I was in the backseat. The car was completely mangled. I had a few cuts, but nothing major." I stop. Louis and Trent are the only people in the world who know the story. I've never actually said it out loud to anyone, until now—when I told it to my archenemy. Oh no.

I look over at Allison. She's looking at me crossly. "I see what you're thinking," she says, and sits down next to me.

"What?"

"It's written all over your face."

"WHAT?"

"I wouldn't do that," she says softly. "Not with this." She reaches up to wipe the tear off my cheek that I didn't even know was there. But then her hand stops, as if she suddenly remembers that, even though we'd known each other for a while, we'd only just met.

Pull it together.

"Didn't you have any relatives?" she asks.

"No. They put me in an orphanage. Right from the start, none of the other kids wanted anything to do with me. They knew I was different. They wouldn't talk to me; they wouldn't play with me. If I tried to join one of their games, everyone else would just quit on the spot. It was obvious they were scared of me. I just remember being lonely and miserable.

"I was six years old, and pretty sure that I was going to spend the rest of my life in that orphanage, when Phantom found me. He said he had been looking all over for someone like me. And I asked, 'Well, what took you so long to find me?'"

She laughs. "Seriously?"

"Yeah." I smile and shrug. "I was six. My attitude was, 'Why couldn't you find me? I was right here!'"

"So he gave you a place to live," she says. "Clothed you, fed you, trained you, put you in the best school in the city, blah, blah, blah . . ."

"Yeah. He gave me a life, gave me purpose . . . I'm indebted to him."

"That's great, but what does that have to do with your awful costume?"

"He wants me to wear it. It's important to him, and it's hard for me to go against that."

She looks at me, studying my face until I get uncomfortable. I wait for the barbed response. She surprises me. "Obligation. I get that. But you've kinda gotta draw the line somewhere, and I would say mortal embarrassment is a pretty good place to draw it."

"Great. Thanks for the advice. And how am I supposed to do that?"

"I think that counts as your question."

"Wha—? Hey! That's no fair! You just asked me a bunch of questions!"

"Then you should've said something," she says with a smile and a shrug. "Sorry, those are the rules,"

"Fine. Then give me an answer."

"OK . . . I know it's hard—trust me—but you've gotta do something. Your outfit is historically awful. I mean, I can't decide which is worse, the front or the back. It's like you're smuggling grapefruits back there."

"And there's the insult."

"Look, when my dad made me come back—"

"He made you come back?"

"Not your turn," she scolds. "When I came back as Monkeywrench, my dad wanted me to wear the same costume I wore when I was eight. Yeah, like that was going to happen. What was I supposed to do with these?" She points to her chest. My eyes widen, and a single bead of sweat forms on my forehead. And then I realize that . . .

"You just asked a question," I gloat. "That was your turn."

"Wha—no!

"Rules of the game."

"Oh MAN! Well played, sir," she says. "OK, smarty . . . so what am I supposed to do with these?" She points to her chest again. She knows how uncomfortable she's making me.

"You could wear a sports bra . . . or I've heard that some ballerinas tape theirs down."

"Tell you what, I'll tape my boobs down when you tape your balls down."

I clear my throat. "Fair enough. No tape, then. Now, I do believe it's my turn."

"Whatever . . . I think I'm all out of tights jokes at the moment, anyway, so go ahead. Even though I think I already know what's coming."

"Why are you a villain?" As I say it, she mouths the words with me. "OK, so I'm obvious. Just answer the question."

"I don't consider myself a villain," she says.

"All right . . . then why are you a sidekick to a villain?"

"I don't think my dad is a villain, either. And I'm not just saying that because he's my dad. Trust me, I'm pretty ticked off at him right now."

I raise an eyebrow. "Why?"

"Guess you'll have to wait for your next turn."

"Fine. You still haven't answered my original question yet."

"All right . . . look, think about all the 'crimes' my father has committed. How many people have actually gotten hurt? Hm? And I'm not talking big businessmen getting financially hit. I'm talking actual people, getting physically hurt. How many?"

I think about it, but I really don't have to. I know the point she's making. "I'm guessing none."

"One. An old security guard had a heart attack a few years ago on that secret soda recipe thing. Remember that?"

I nodded. It was a long time ago, but I remembered. Can-do Cola had some secret, new-flavor formula they were trying to protect. They said it was going to revolutionize the entire soda industry. "Yeah, your dad was trying to steal that soda recipe so he could sell it on the black market."

"What?! Where'd you hear that?"

"Oh, come on! What else would he want it for?"

"Uhh, hello? Disgustingly unhealthy new soda, destined to create a whole new generation of morbidly obese children, and a corporation that only cared about the money it was going to make them. He was going to destroy it."

"Bull. He did it for the money!"

She laughs dismissively. "Yeah, I don't think so. My dad's a plus intelligence. You know how many patents he has? A ton. Trust me, money is not a problem."

"OK . . . if you say so."

"I can tell you don't believe me, but I don't care. I'm continuing my story. So . . . anyway . . . the poor, old security guard was only a couple of days from retirement when he had his heart attack, of course," she says. "So what did the company do? They fired him! The big jerks slashed his pension in half! They said that because of his incompetence, we almost got away with that stupid secret formula."

I laugh. "They made such a big deal about that garbage."

"I know! Did you try it?"

"Yeah. It was horrible. Tasted like melted cherry lollipops."

"Right? Bleh . . . soooo sweet," she says. "Anyway, when my dad found out the guard couldn't work again, he ended up paying the guy's hospital bills. Then he stuck a couple mil in his bank account . . . anonymously, of course."

"Bull."

"I have the bank statement at home to prove it. Trust me, if I didn't see that statement, I wouldn't believe it, either."

"All right . . . even if your dad did give money to a guy who had a heart attack because of him, that still doesn't excuse the fact that he's a criminal. He steals stuff. He destroys stuff that isn't his. He threatens the safety of every person in this city."

"No, he doesn't. He threatens the safety of every *corporation* in the city. Big difference."

"No, there isn't. Corporations are legal. Even if your dad *is* stealing stuff from them just to destroy it, it's still illegal."

"You are so naive! Corporations are the ones that are evil and greedy and don't care who they hurt! They use their money and power to bully people, and people don't even realize it! They get away with murder! Literally! And people don't care! My dad tries to make them care. Or at least open their eyes to what's going on."

"Look . . . even if that is true—and I don't think it is—there are LEGAL ways to do that."

She laughs. "Puh-leeeze. The law is a joke. It's bought and sold every day on the open market. And who does the buying? The guys with all the money. And what do they buy? Their ability to do whatever they want without anyone bothering them."

"Then go after them with the law! Use your powers to expose them legally!"

"They're too powerful and crafty!"

"Then try harder!"

Somehow, we're standing face-to-face, our faces an inch apart. When she yells at me, I can smell her gum: cinnamon, spicy. My stomach does a little flip, like the first time I jumped off a building. I take a step back. I have to remember my mission . . . stay close to her. This may be a little too close.

"Sorry I was yelling," I say.

Her eyes have dropped away from me, and she's looking at the gargoyle. Maybe I'm imagining things, but she looks nervous all of a sudden. "It's OK. Bound to happen sooner or later. We are archenemies, y'know." She looks at me and smiles. My stomach flips again, and I realize I'm holding my breath. I let it go and smile back at her. What is my problem? "OK, mortal enemy . . . my turn. Do you ever feel lonely?"

"What?!" I start laughing. "No."

"Really . . . because every time I see you, you look lonely."

"Um, excuse me, but aren't you the girl who didn't even recognize me last night?"

"I recognized you. I just didn't know your name."

"Isn't knowing someone's name the definition of recognizing someone?"

"Shut up." She laughs. "You know what I mean. I knew you. My friends and I called you That Lonely Kid . . . when we weren't calling you Steve, that is."

"Awesome. That makes me feel much better."

"So . . . answer the question."

"Yeah, I guess. But doesn't everyone?"

She rolls her eyes at me. "Not an 'Oh, my friends aren't here, so I'm a little lonely today,' kinda way. More of an 'I don't connect with people at all ever' kinda way."

"I don't know."

"That's a yes."

"No, that's an 'I don't know.'"

"If it was a no, you'd know it. Since you don't know, it's a yes."

"What are you, an evil supershrink?" I ask.

"HA! I love it! Maybe I'll transition from Monkey-wrench to Evil Supershrink over the next couple of years. Now THAT'S going to be a hard costume to design."

"Well, wait . . . what about you? Aren't you lonely?"

"There's your turn."

"Fine, it's my turn. Answer the question."

"No, I'm not. Not anymore. Unlike you, I actually made an effort to make friends."

"Yeah, but they don't know you. I mean they know you, Allison Mendes, but they don't know you, Monkeywrench, evil sidekick."

"OK, first, you need to put the brakes on the whole 'evil' thing. We settled that. It's dead. Got it, Bright Buns?"

"Well, I thought we settled the costume thing, yet there you go with the whole Bright Buns thing again . . ."

"We did. I just had to get one last one in. Mm-kay?"

"Whatever."

"OK, on to your yet another completely naive point. No, my friends don't know that I'm Monkeywrench. I mean, God, can you imagine?" She changes her posture ever so slightly, and her face scrunches, like she just ate a whole lemon. "Come on, girls," she says in her screechy,

Monkeywrench voice, "let's go see a movie this weekend! Ha-ha-ha-ha-ha-ha-ha!"

I cringe. "Gahh. I hear that voice in my nightmares. And is that what your face looks like under the mask when you're doing it?"

"Shut up! You are the last person that should be poking fun at someone's superhero appearance."

"Careful . . ."

"Or what?"

"Evil!" I yell.

"Buns!" she yells.

We're both laughing hard now. "I always knew you were a big jerk," she says.

"No, you always knew Bright Boy was a big jerk. Me, you had no idea."

"Fine . . . my point is that you're the only person who knows completely who you are. Everyone else sees a side of you. My dad sees me one way, my teachers see me another, my friends—"

"Me."

She pauses. "You . . . see me another way."

"It's funny," I say, "but out of everyone we know, we're the ones who sees the most sides of each other." It was meant to be an offhand comment, but the minute I said it, we both felt it. It had the weight of truth.

"Everyone has different sides to their personality," she says, trying to lighten the moment. "Except Jake Berkshire."

"Ugh, what an idiot."

"Yeah, I'm pretty sure that guy's only operating on one level."

"Barely," I say. "You know it's a constant struggle for me to not kick the ever-lovin' snot out of him? Every day, I have to tell myself it's a no-win situation. But, man, would it feel good to just unleash on him."

She gives me a sly, sideways smile.

"What?" I ask her.

"Nothing. It's just . . . I guess I always thought you were going to be this huge weenie. . . not you 'you', Bright Boy, you . . ."

"Yeah, I got it."

"It's a pleasant surprise."

"What is?"

"That you're more of a dork than a weenie."

"You give the worst compliments, you know that?"

"Is that your question?"

"Yes, it was," I say, "and you asking if that was my question was yours."

"Argh!"

"My turn! My question is why are you angry at your dad, apart from him being a villain and all?"

She gives me a playful slap on the arm.

"Ow!" I say, rubbing my arm.

"You're actually not completely wrong. I am mad because of the whole *villain* thing, but not the way you think." She takes a deep breath. "I spent my whole childhood friendless, missing out on all the stuff that normal kids do, all because my dad wanted to take down some evil corporations, which I still respect, you know? No, you don't know," she says before I can respond. "It's just . . . I have a normal life now . . . somewhat . . . and he has to pop up out of nowhere and dredge all this stuff up again. I agree with his message—I just wish he could deliver it without the tights."

"Well, you know—"

"If you're about to say, 'Then why don't you go straight?' you might as well save it, OK? Not going to happen."

"Fine. I guess we'll just have to remain mortal enemies."

"Fine." She grabs my arm in excitement. "OK, my turn!"

"Shoot."

There's that sly smile again, the one that gives my stomach a workout . . . the one I have a hard time looking away from. "Want me to help you pick out a new outfit?"

11

"COME OUT OF THERE AND LET ME SEE,"

she calls from outside the dressing room.

I'm in the only dressing room in the back of Jimmy's Army/Navy Surplus Store, looking into a mirror at a kid I don't recognize. He looks like a much cooler version of me.

"Come on!!" she yells.

"You pick this stuff out just to set me up?" I ask. "So you can knock me around a little easier?"

"Oh, puh-leeeze. I don't need any help knocking you around. Now step out here before I prove it."

I step out. Allison stares at me.

"Are you OK?" I ask.

"Huh?"

"I think it looks all right," I say tentatively.

"You idiot. You look AMAZING."

It's all navy blue, formfitting, but not in a prima ballerina way, more like a really cool woven leather–type outfit. But it doesn't look like a jumpsuit or a pair of tights anymore; it looks more like a combat outfit. There are a few bright yellow and orange highlights . . . just enough to justify the Bright Boy name, but not enough to be too tacky. It's worlds away from the deranged circus outfit I'm used to wearing.

"So . . . do you like it?" she asks.

"It's perfect." I run my hands across the sleeves. "What is this stuff?"

"I call it python scales. My own design," Jimmy says, coming out of his office. He's a short guy with REALLY hairy arms. He looks like he's been through a few wars. "Leather over ceramic plates, plus a fabric of my own design."

"It's amazing," I say. "It's so light. I hardly feel it at all. Will it stand up to . . . uhh . . ."

"Martial arts practicing. That *is* what you're using it for, right?" he says.

"Right."

"Yeah, it should stand up to that. It'll stop a .44

Magnum hollow-point from about ten feet away. You'll have a heck of a bruise, but you'll make it. If you're practicing martial arts in a really bad neighborhood, that is."

"Right."

"Yeah, well, I don't sell that to just anyone off the street, you know. That's special stock. You're a friend of Allison's, so . . ."

"Thanks."

"Yeah, thanks, Jimmy," Allison says, giving him a small kiss on the cheek. "You're a genius. I owe you."

"Not if you pay for it, you don't," he says. He gives her a little smile and wink, then slips back into his office and closes the door.

I lean in to Allison. "Does he know we're—?"

"Yeah, probably, but he never says. He'll make a comment or two, but then just goes back into his office. Jimmy really is a genius, though, so I'm pretty sure we're not the first plus/pluses to come around looking for costumes."

"Yeah . . . hey, what do you think happened to all the other plus/pluses?" I ask.

"Don't know."

"I mean, supposedly before we were born, the city was

full of them. According to a couple of things I read, you couldn't fall off a building without three supers fighting over who was going to save you. Even when I was just starting out, there were still plenty around. Now it's just Phantom and me, and like a handful of villains."

She raises her hand to slap my arm, but I literally beat her to the punch. "And you and your dad, who aren't villains, just misunderstood people that the public calls villains because they're lazy," I say, all in one breath.

"Nicely done," she says.

"So, don't you think it's weird that the plus/plus population basically disappeared?"

Allison shrugs. "I don't know. Maybe they all just got sick of living their lives for other people."

"Yeah . . . maybe some of the drop-off was because some of them got old, or went to jail, or just decided to go do something else . . . but what happened to all the pluses around our age?" I ask. "They never showed up."

"Maybe they don't have your 'strong sense of justice,'" she says in a slightly mocking voice.

"I guess. Still think it's weird." I feel a little distance between us starting to form, so I let it drop. I look at myself in the mirror again. "You sure I look OK?"

"Fishing for compliments?"

"No, it's just . . . I think I look OK, but I see people dressed like idiots all the time, and I assume that they think they look OK, too, so . . ."

"You don't have anything to worry about. Turn around," she says.

I do as instructed, giving her a little wiggle. She laughs. "Careful. Don't let it go to your head." She looks me up and down. "Much better. Hot, but tasteful. You leave a little to the imagination, now. So how do you feel?"

"Amazing. Like I'm tough . . . a good guy, still, but . . . you know . . ." I do a few jumps. My head almost hits the ceiling.

"Whoa," Allison says. "Take it easy."

"I can move. It breathes."

"Yeah. I get all my stuff here. My dad has no idea and it drives him nuts. He wants me to wear the costumes he makes for me." She stops, as if something new just occurred to her. "In fact, come on."

She drags me toward the register and pulls out her credit card. She pulls the tags off my new outfit and hands them to the middle-aged cashier, who looks like she's barely functioning. "Here's the tags. He's going to wear the clothes out of the store," she says. "Cool?"

"What are you doing?" I ask.

"Sshh . . . I love the idea of Dr. Chaotic buying Bright Boy's new costume," she whispers in my ear. Goose bumps run up the back of my neck. She pulls back and smiles at me. My mind is racing to try to figure out what to say so that she'll have to whisper in my ear again, but all I can do is grin at her like an idiot.

The cashier hands Allison the receipt, as if ringing us up was the only thing keeping her awake. I grab Allison by the shoulders and present her to the cashier. "You know, this girl is Monkeywrench."

"You jerk!" Allison yells, but she's laughing. "Well, this is Bright Boy, and thanks to me, he doesn't look like a pervert anymore."

"Hey!"

The cashier looks at us without saying a word. Her expression doesn't change. This causes us to laugh even harder. Allison punches my arm and runs for the door.

"Come on, Bright Boy!"

"Coming, Monkeywrench!" We run out the door, laughing.

It's evening now. We run three blocks at regular human speed. Suddenly, Allison turns on her plus speed and darts into an alley.

"Costume stash," she says. "Turn around."

"I look like an idiot, standing in front of an alley like this." I start to turn to look at her.

"Hey! I'm half-dressed here!"

"Sorry," I turn back. I can feel the blood rushing to my face.

"OK. You can turn around now."

I do. She's dressed in her Monkeywrench costume, but a different version of it, one that isn't designed to hide the fact that she's a girl. She looks sleek and beautiful, and I can't believe someone who looks like that is actually talking to me. "What do you think?" she asks. "I've been working on it for the past couple of weeks."

"You look like a girl."

"Yeah. That's the point. My dad has been against it, but I'm tired of hiding it."

"You—" I stop. I'm blushing; I can feel it. I look down at my shoes. I can't look her in the eyes and say it. "You look amazing."

"Thanks," she says. I look up to see that she's now blushing, too. "I figured since you were taking a chance with a new outfit, maybe I should . . . you know . . . give it a run . . . see how it feels."

"This is—"

"Crazy? I agree," she says. "You need a mask. I always keep a couple around. Here." She flips me one. I put it on. "You ready, Bright Boy?"

"Wait—"

"No. No time for waiting. Catch me and win a prize." She smiles at me, then grabs onto the fire escape overhead and hoists herself up. She scales the metal bars and, in the blink of an eye, she's standing on the roof. She looks down on me, her expression full of joy and mischief. "Come on! Don't keep a girl waiting!"

I smile at her, then leap, grabbing onto the fire escape more than half of the way up. She takes off as I'm climbing to the roof. I hit the roof and give chase.

She sprints toward the edge and leaps without hesitating, easily crossing the thirty feet between buildings. I do the same. I can hear her laughter in front of me, echoing through the streets. She leaps for the next roof, but this time she spreads her arms wide, as if she's going to start gliding around the city . . . but then she tucks her legs under her and does a front somersault. She lands on the roof of the next building, sprinting without breaking stride.

I run and watch her leap gracefully over chimneys, flip effortlessly over air conditioners, fly across the blank space between buildings, and I wonder if this is what regular people feel when they watch us: the feeling that nothing else in this world could possibly move and fly and leap and laugh so effortlessly. I want to watch her fly across rooftops forever.

She looks back at me. I can see the gleam of neon and streetlights reflected in her eyes. "Hey, slowpoke!"

I laugh. I still have a couple of gears left, so I slip into one and gain some ground on her. She turns around and I'm almost on top of her. "HEY!" She tries to speed up. But she's too late. I put my hand on her shoulder. She grabs it, and, using her forward momentum, flips me over. A split second after she releases me, I'm already adjusting midair. I land on my feet, ready to go.

"Ooooo," she says. "Bright Boy wants to play?"

I nod.

"Too cool to speak," she laughs. "Looks like I've created a monster."

"You going to talk, or are you going to fight?"

She smiles at me, then follows it up with a roundhouse kick to my head. I drop forward onto my stomach to avoid the kick, then try to sweep her leg. She does an evasive little hop, then falls on top of me. I'm no longer sure I want to continue the fight. I have a moment where

I wonder if she's starting to think the same thing. Then she whispers in my ear, "We're still fighting." With that, she puts both hands under my chin and pulls my head back. I push myself up into a standing position, so that she's now riding me piggyback style. I run backward, knowing that there's a chimney behind me at ten paces. Apparently, she knows it, too, because just before impact, she climbs onto my shoulders and does a front flip off of me. I slam my butt into the chimney, chipping away some of the brick.

"That looked like it hurt," she says.

"It tickled." I lunge at her with a right hook, but it's only a feint, used to set up a scissor kick. She manages to grab my foot midair, but I use my other foot to knock her hand off.

It's like we're dancing across rooftops, perfectly in sync with each other . . . laughing through the punches and the kicks and the blocks and the counters.

She kicks me off the roof of one building, but FP-769 is right there. I flip off it and land on the top of a parked cargo truck. She comes flying in after me and I somehow manage to catch her in a bear hug. I clasp my hands together and keep her off the ground so that she can't get any leverage. She tries to struggle free, so I start tickling her.

"Ha-ha-ha-ha-ha-ha-ha-stop-it-ha-ha-ha-ha-ha!"

"I caught you! Say uncle! Say uncle!"

"Uncle! Aunt! Freakin' cousins, just stop tickling MEEEE!!"

I stop tickling and put her down, but I don't let go. She stops struggling, stops moving. She looks up at me. "You said something about a prize?" I say.

She puts her hand behind my head, pulls me in, and kisses me. Her lips are salty. I smell cinnamon and flowers. I can hear my heartbeat in my temples. Then I realize that it isn't my heartbeat. We stop kissing, then peer over the side of the truck. About seventy-five people are standing there applauding. At least ten of them are filming us with their phones.

We start laughing. Allison waves and blows kisses.

"We're dead," I say, but I'm still laughing. I can't help it.

"No, we're not. Not yet, at least," she says. She blows another kiss to the crowd, which is now cheering. She looks at me. She kisses her fingers, then places those fingers gently on my lips. I hold her hand there for a second, and then it's gone. She's backflipped onto the roof of a passing truck. "See you in school tomorrow!" she calls out. I watch her until she's out of sight.

He pulls the honey out of the cabinet and slides it across the counter to me. "So . . . where were you yesterday?"

My eyes go wide for a split second. I try to go back to being nonchalant, but I know it's no use. Louis saw. He always sees. If he wasn't our caretaker, I think he'd be a detective of some sort, one who secretly makes the world's most perfect pancakes.

"Do you want time to think of a lie," he asks, "or do you wanna try your luck?"

"I was out."

"I know you were out, that's why I asked where you were."

"Uh-huh."

"So?"

"I was walking around the city. I figure I spend so much time flipping off of rooftops, I might as well check it out from the sidewalk, you know?"

"So . . . you went walking . . . around the city . . . by yourself."

"Well, not exactly."

Louis laughs. I smile and shake my head. Getting anything past Louis is an impossibility. "What's her name?"

"I don't . . . It's . . . I'm not even sure she . . . uh . . ."

"Yeah, well, don't hurt yourself," he says. "I just hope to God that my life never depends on you keeping a secret."

Yeah, that one hits a little too close to home. "Come on," I say, dropping my fork and grabbing my backpack. "I don't want to be late."

Louis raises an eyebrow. "Well, well, well . . . look who's suddenly anxious to get to school."

One of the great things about Louis is his ability to know when I want to be left alone. The drive to school is quiet. I try not to get my hopes up. Yesterday was yesterday. Allison and I had a great time. OK, an AMAZING time. And really, all I can think about is the next time I get to spend all day with her . . . but we are enemies. MAJOR enemies, in a constant battle that will never end until one of us is dead or in jail. Plus, she may not even really like me. I'm just going to assume that she regrets what happened last night and go from there. Let her make the first move.

When we pull up to the school, I notice right away that something is different. Louis doesn't seem to notice, but then why would he? He has no idea what goes on at my school.

"Good luck, kid," he says, and gives me a smile like he's amused and delighted and wants to be supportive. It may be the best smile I've ever seen from him.

"Thanks." I get out and close the door. Louis gives me a little wave as he drives off. I can feel the energy of my classmates on my back; I turn to face it. They're all buzzing around the front steps, giddy and chatty and barely under control. Something tells me it's about Bright Boy.

"Did you see it?" one girl squeals to her friends, and instantly my heart sinks.

Oh my God, my fly was open. Had to be. I go to all the trouble of getting a new outfit, and then I do something stupid like forget to zip up, and I'm going to spend the rest of my life being called a freak and a perv—

"Oh. MY. GOD! THEY ARE SO AWESOME!" another girl screeches.

OK, now I have no idea what they're talking about.

"He is SOOO hot! Can you believe it?"

"I KNOW! I swear, I had no idea it was him, and then he looked at that one guy and was like, 'I'm Bright Boy.'" She then makes a sound that I had never heard a girl make before. I swear it's part feline.

Another girl joins their conversation. "And that's Monkeywrench!"

"I KNOOOW!" the two other girls yell in unison.

"But they're enemies!"

"She's a villain!"

"I KNOW!" The two girls look at the phone of the third. The sound of the video she's playing attracts ten more kids who happen to be passing at the moment, like a magnet pulling in iron filings. I blend into this crowd and try to get a look at the video.

It's shaky, but clear. There I am . . . there's Allison. We're flipping and fighting, and it all comes rushing back to me. My face tingles; my heart speeds up. I can feel the energy as more kids filter over, until the video Allison and the video me kiss, and the crowd cheers, not just in the video, but the kids around me right now, watching.

"Monkeywrench is a girl?" someone shouts.

"You bet she is," I almost say, but decide to keep it to myself.

One of our teachers, Ms. Stanfield, comes to the front door. "I hate to interrupt this community gathering, but it would be nice if we could give your parents their money's worth today. Let's go. Inside. Start gathering into your groups."

Everyone starts filtering in through the doors. The girl with the video on her phone is right in front of me.

When she passes, Ms. Stanfield whispers to her, "Is that from last night?"

The girl nods, not sure if she's about to get in trouble for it.

"Which one is it?" Ms. Stanfield asks.

The girl's eyes light up. "Evan Rodriguez's."

"I haven't seen that one yet!" And now Ms. Stanfield is practically squealing. "Oh my God, when do you have some free time?"

"Third period."

"Perfect! I'll be in my room. Come find me." The girl and teacher nod excitedly at each other.

What is going on?

Something grabs me and pulls me into darkness. I'm in the same closet as before, and once again, I'm looking at Allison. My breath catches. She looks beautiful.

"What is going on around here?" I ask. "And you really have a thing for this closet, huh?"

"Pretty wild, right?" she says. Her cheeks are flush with color. "Not the closet . . . the whole video thing. Looks like we're a hit."

"Seriously?"

"Uh . . . yeah! All the kids are talking about it . . . even the boys. And boys don't usually go for that stuff."

"What stuff?"

"You know . . . the mushy stuff," she says, and looks down at her shoes.

I can feel the blood rushing to my face. "Uhh . . . do you . . . uh"—I don't want to say it, but I force myself to— "regret . . . it?"

"What? The kiss? Yes. I woke up this morning and thought to myself, Oh my God, I can't believe I kissed that loser!"

"Oh."

She steps in close to me, reaches up, and pulls my head close to hers. "And I can't believe I'm about to do it again." She kisses me. Her lips are soft and taste like peppermint today. "What is wrong with me?" She whispers as we stop. She's staring into my eyes. She nibbles on her bottom lip and smiles, and every nerve ending in my body goes electric.

"What are we doing?" I whisper back.

"You mean you don't know? I knew you were innocent, but I thought you'd at least know what making out is."

"Not that. I mean, that, but not like that . . . you know . . . we're enemies! We're going to have to fight each other! Probably tonight!"

"So?"

"SO?! I don't want to fight you anymore."

She smiles. "Why not? We fought last night and it turned out OK."

I take a deep breath and let it out slowly. A million things are going through my mind. I think of my duty to the city, my commitment to Phantom Justice . . . and what I'm feeling for this girl in front of me right now, and all I want to do is leave all that hero/villain stuff behind.

"Listen," she says, "I know all the reasons why this can't possibly work are running through your head right now, but stop. You like me . . . I think . . ."

I nod until my head almost falls off. "Do you?"

She laughs. "Yes, I like you, too."

I smile, relieved.

"So let's just keep it simple. You like me; I like you. My God, we're like Romeo and Juliet! With superpowers!"

"Allison, they die in the end."

"Yeah, because they didn't have secret identities. Or superstrength. Look, we'll figure this out, OK? In the meantime." She kisses me quickly on the lips, then punches me hard in the arm.

"OW! What the—?!"

"Tag. You're it." And with that, she slips out the door. I open the door a split second later, but she's already gone. Oh, this is not over.

Two classes later, in English, I get up to go to the bathroom, and even though Ms. Stanfield is looking right at me, I punch Allison in the arm as I pass by her. The punch is so fast that no one sees it. Allison rubs her arm and looks at me, amused, annoyed, and impressed. She scrunches her face up in a "Oh, you're in for it, mister" expression. I wink at her before slipping out the door.

While I'm standing in line at lunch, Allison slips in and nails me. My hamburger almost hits the kid in front of me. I grin all the way through lunch. The kids at my table look at me like I'm an idiot, but as per usual, no one says anything.

I get Allison again with the "heading off to the bathroom" trick in math class, but this time she's ready for me, and as soon as I tag her, she tags me right back. The teacher walks over to the window and looks out at the clear blue sky.

"Huh," she says. "Thought I heard thunder."

Meanwhile, all anyone can talk about, kids and teachers alike, is what is going on between Bright Boy and Monkeywrench? When did he change costumes? When did she become a she? When did they start chasing each other around the city, kissing? Yesterday, yesterday, and yesterday, I mentally answer. For the first time in years, I feel good about both of my selves. I feel like I have a secret worth having again, and oddly enough, it makes it easier to keep.

I head to seventh-period. Allison sits a couple of seats over from me. Her friends, Olivia and Charlene, come in, but Allison isn't with them. So . . . if she's been called out of school, then that means—

"Will Scott Hutchinson please report to the office? Scott Hutchinson."

I'm already halfway down the hall by the second "Scott Hutchinson." I'm excited, giddy, anxious to see—

"Hello, sissy boy."

Standing in front of me, blocking my path, are Jake and his three meathead friends.

"Shouldn't you guys be in class?" I ask.

The question seems to baffle them.

"Are you talking to us?" Jake asks. "You're not allowed to talk to us, sissy boy. You hear me?" His friends laugh.

I don't have time for this. I look around the hallway. Except for them and me, the place is deserted. A strange calm comes over me. "I'll talk to whoever I want, including you and your idiot friends. Got it, Jake?" Jake's mouth swings open like a trapdoor. "Oh, and call me sissy boy one more time, and you and your buddies will be waking up an hour from now, right here, wondering what just happened. *Capisce?*"

For a second, I see something like worry pass over Jake's face, but then it's gone. He steps forward and puts his face a half inch from mine. His breath is unexpectedly minty. "Sissy. Boy."

I smile, crack my neck left, then right. Before Jake can even think to react, I hit him with an open left hand. I pull my slap at the last second, so as not to give him any permanent damage. He goes flying across the hall. His friends only have a moment to watch before I'm on them. I sweep Jimmy Douglas's legs out from under him. Then I grab the front of Shane McConaughey's shirt and pull him toward me, swirl him through a modified jiujitsu move, then send him sprawling on top of Jake. Andrew Buckley just stands there with his eyes wide, his mouth open, and his hands up. "Boo," I say, and flick my hand open; he sprints away down the hall.

"See you boys later," I say, then head to the office. For some reason, I start whistling.

As I expect, Louis is there, looking somber. As he tells the secretary the story of some dying aunt, I sigh impatiently.

"OK," I say after he wraps it up. "So are we going?"

"Uh. Yeah. Right away."

"Uh-huh," says the secretary behind the desk, who doesn't seem to be listening to any of this. "Make sure you sign out please."

"Yeah, you bet," Louis says. He signs the sheet of paper on the clipboard, and we're on our way.

Louis is not looking at me as we walk. He's keeping a pace that, for someone with no abilities, is a little fast.

"Something big happen?" I ask.

He doesn't say anything until we're outside the school.

"What do you think you're doing?" he asks without breaking pace.

"What do you mean?"

"In that office. I'm talking about your dying aunt, and you act like you couldn't care less."

"She wasn't even listening."

"That's not the point! This is about keeping your cover. What if she *was* listening?"

"Come on, Louis," I say. "Kids get pulled out of class all the time. Plus, I've been down to that office a dozen times since school started. It's a wonder I have any 'relatives' left to kill off. If you were worried about being conspicuous, you might want to either drop the 'dying relative' stories or think about homeschooling."

"Yeah, OK. I see. I get it. You don't have to worry about such things as excuses and identities anymore. You've found love, right? And now the whole world knows about it."

Uh-oh.

"And love conquers all, right? Is that what we're talking about here?"

"You saw the video," I say. My heart speeds up, and I feel a little nauseous.

"Get in the car."

I do as I'm told.

Louis gets behind the wheel without saying another word. He peels out.

"Hey!" some guy on the ground calls up to me. "Hey!"

"Yeah?"

"Who are you?"

I smile. "I'm Bright Boy." I leap off the truck and disappear into the night.

1 2

"SCOTT?"

I can hear Louis calling my name, but I'm not ready to answer him. I'm too busy playing over the movie my brain made of last night: the leaping across rooftops, the fighting, the kiss . . . On command, my stomach does a flop.

"Trying to move the carton of the orange juice with your mind?" Louis asks. He slides the plate of freshly made pancakes in front of me. They're so perfect they look fake, like they were made out of plastic for a pancake ad. Louis takes his pancakes seriously.

"Sorry," I say. "Lost in thought there for a second."

"Yeah, I got that. Syrup or honey?"

"Honey, please."

lot. I know that. But I have to take a stand on this. That costume is embarrassing."

"Would you stop with the costume for one second?!" he yells. Louis never yells. "There is more at stake here than your stupid costume!"

"What do you mean by that?"

Louis takes a deep breath, but then doesn't say anything.

"Louis?"

"Nothing," he says, trying to sound angry again, but not quite pulling it off. "We're home."

We sit in the car for a moment. I look at him in the rearview mirror, but he doesn't look back.

I put my hand on the door handle.

"Sorry for snapping at you, kid," he says.

"It's OK. I screwed up. I guess I expected some sort of scolding. I just didn't think it would come from you."

There's a long pause. Finally, Louis says, "Good luck."

I open the door and get out. He pulls the car around the circular driveway and disappears toward the garage.

I walk inside and head up to my room to change. I look around. Nothing is out of place, but something seems wrong, as if someone went to a lot of trouble to

169

make it feel like no one was in here. Or maybe I'm just being paranoid. I'm too wound up to know the difference right now.

I pull my new costume out of the duffel bag I carry to school and get dressed as quickly as possible. I'm about to check it out in the mirror when I stop. What if it was Allison's plan all along to befriend me, make me "stand up for myself," cause strife between me and Phantom, then use that strife to divide and defeat us?

Of course! I feel like an idiot for not seeing it before. It's probably better to take the stupid thing off right now, go down to the Fortress, and talk this out with Trent. Who knows? Maybe we can come up with a new costume together.

I take off the mask and throw it on the bed. I'm starting to take off the shirt when I look up and see myself in the full-length mirror . . . I look better than I ever imagined I could look. Allison may be setting me up, but she hasn't put me in a stupid-looking costume to do it. At least I know the fight I'm about to have with Trent will be worth it, just on fashion sense alone. I put my shirt back on and head downstairs.

My hand is shaking as I hit the hidden button that

moves the bookcase concealing the main entrance to the Fortress. I'm a little queasy as I go through the security measures, even screwing up once and having to reset before the stun lasers knock me unconscious. By the time I get to the retina scan, I'm pretty nerved up. The scan registers on the third try, and I enter the Fortress.

Trent is sitting with his back toward me, in front of the computer bay. He doesn't turn around. He knows I'm here. There are cameras in the security corridor leading down here, and the images from them are on the monitors.

I clear my throat a couple of times, but Trent still doesn't turn around. The awkwardness is making me even more antsy. I keep rubbing my sweaty palms on the front of my pants, but the material isn't absorbent.

Finally, I find my voice. "Uhh . . . so . . . is Dr. Chaotic up to something?" I ask.

"He's at IGO Computer headquarters," Phantom says in his annoying whisper-growl. "Your uniform is in the car. You can change on the way."

"I'm already dressed," I say. My heart is thudding in my chest. I'd rather be yelling at a gun-wielding maniac than talking to Phantom Justice about my new outfit.

"I see. Would it happen to be the same outfit you were wearing when you were making out with your archenemy?" he asks. He still won't turn around.

"We weren't making out," I mumble. "It was just a kiss." Even I know that defense sounds lame.

"Well . . . that's *much* better," he says sarcastically. "I can see why you'd want to clarify that. Come on then . . . let's get a look at this amazing new outfit." He swivels his chair around. "OK . . . there's no way in hell you're going out dressed like that."

"Uhh . . . yes, I am."

"Uhh . . . no, you're not. You look ridiculous . . . like a rank amateur, a weekend warrior out for thrills."

"No, I don't," I say, but my self-confidence is eroding. I start to sweat.

"And whose stupid idea was it to put you in dark blue when your name is Bright Boy? Hm?"

"Did you just call me stupid?" I ask.

"I don't know. Did I? Did you actually choose a dark blue outfit when your name is Bright Boy?"

"You're right. Putting me in bright yellow tights is a much smarter costume choice."

He's up and in my face in half a second. Even as fast as I am, that was fast. "You didn't just say what I think you said, did you?"

"Trent—"

"You didn't just imply that I'm the stupid one in this scenario, did you?"

"Trent, I—"

"Maybe you have a problem wearing tights because you're a pervert. Hm? Did you ever think of that?"

I blush. It's something that I've been wrestling with since it happened, and Trent just slapped me in the face with it. "I couldn't help it," I mumble as I turn away from him.

"Just like you couldn't help making out with your enemy? Huh? You're supposed to be my sidekick? How am I supposed to trust you when you can't even control yourself?"

My jaw tightens. Even though I may be wrong, and I could have handled things a little better, Trent is being a jerk . . . and it's starting to tick me off.

"I swear to God, Scott. Sometimes, you can be so stupid! Did you ever think that she was setting you up? Huh? That somehow, she bugged that outfit, and now she knows who you are?"

"She already knows who I am."

"And who's fault is that?!" he yells. "You're acting like an idiot! And an amateur!" He gets in my face again. His jaw is clenched in fury. "I will not let you ruin this for me, do you understand? I have spent too much time, worked too hard to build this, and you are not going to screw it up. Do you understand?! Now get in the car and put on your tights!"

I stare at him. I'd seen him go off on villains before, but I always got the sense that his anger—his violence—was controlled. It didn't feel controlled right now. But it didn't matter. I'd come this far, and there was no way I was going to turn back.

"No," I say. I try to speak calmly, but my voice keeps shaking. "I can't put those on again. They're embarrassing."

Trent's clenched fists start shaking. My instincts start going into overdrive. I feel my body preparing to go into defense mode. "Scott, I'm only going to say this one more time. Get in the car—"

"No."

"And put on—"

"NO."

"SCOTT! GET IN THE CAR RIGHT NOW AND PUT YOUR DAMN TIGHTS ON!" Trent raises his hand as if he's going to slap me. I snap into a fighting stance and raise my fist on instinct. Do I avoid his slap? Block it? Hit him back?

"Hey!" Louis shouts as he walks into the room. "Dr. Chaotic's on the news!"

Trent's hand is suspended in midair. He looks at Louis. Louis holds his gaze.

"Dr. Chaotic and Monkeywrench are at the IGO Computer headquarters," Louis informs us. "It's all over the news. Looks like they're waiting for you."

Louis and Trent continue to stare at each other. Trent's hand is still up as if he's going to slap me at any moment, even though I've long since moved out of its range. It seems more symbolic, now. If Trent's embarrassed for getting caught, he's not showing it.

After what seems like forever, Trent drops his eyes from Louis's glare. "You know what?" Trent growls. "Wear your stupid outfit. I don't care. Just get in the car." He turns away from me, his cape making a dramatic sweep as he does. He stomps off toward the Stealth Phantom, gets in, and slams the door shut. He revs the engine impatiently. The sound is deafening. For a second, I think he's going to peel out and leave me standing here, but he doesn't. He revs the engine a couple of more times, then sits there idling, staring through the windshield at the far wall so he doesn't have to look at me.

I walk on shaky legs over to the car, open the door, and get in. Before I can get the door closed, Trent hits the gas and backs out at eighty mph. I just manage to get the door shut before it gets snapped off in the tunnel. I catch one last look at Louis as we leave. He looks worried, and I'm not sure it has anything to do with Dr. Chaotic.

14

THE RIDE TO IGO COMPUTER HEADQUARTERS

lasts all of eight minutes. There has never been a longer eight minutes in the history of time. Phantom won't look at me, or acknowledge my presence in any way.

We pull up to the building, and Phantom is out of the car before it even comes to a full stop. By the time I get up to the roof, he's already started his "confrontation dialogue" with Dr. Chaotic, but it sounds stiff and unnatural.

"I don't know what evil you're up to now, Chaotic," Phantom says in a monotone, "but it ends tonight."

"Please. Like you and your brat are going to stop us," Chaotic says, also in a monotone. Dr. Chaotic isn't even looking at Phantom; he's staring at me, and it's making me uncomfortable. He hardly acknowledged my existence before. And now he's not taking his eyes off me.

"Hey!" Phantom yells.

Chaotic looks at me for a couple of seconds more, then finally over at Phantom.

"That's better," Phantom says.

I look at Allison/Monkeywrench. She mouths the word *sorry*.

My eyes go wide. I mouth, *You told him?* That's why he was staring at me.

She makes some faces that indicate no, she did not tell him, you idiot (meaning me), that the video was, in fact, ALL OVER THE INTERNET, and he happened to stumble across it.

Oh. I nod my head in the direction of Phantom Justice, admitting that he kind of did the same thing. She sticks her tongue out at me. I start laughing.

I stop laughing when I notice that Phantom Justice and Dr. Chaotic are no longer talking to each other and are now staring at us.

It's a little awkward.

"Uhh . . . OK . . ." Allison says. "So, the deal is that

we have this prototype of a super computer thingee!"
She tries to ramp it up again so that we can get back on
script, so to speak.

"You don't even know what you're stealing?" I ask.

"Yeah, I do!" she says, annoyed. "It's that thingee."
She points to a box in Dr. Chaotic's hand. He does not
look happy.

"Well!" I shout, trying to pick up on Allison's cue.
"We are here to stop you! Ha-HA!"

Allison looks at me as like "What are you doing?"

"What?"

She laughs and rolls her eyes, then springs forward
and tackles me. "Hey!" I shout. Phantom and Chaotic
look like they're about to break us up when a news
helicopter comes out of nowhere. They hesitate, but
then they start to fight.

I can't watch them, though, because Allison is
coming at me with a barrage of kicks and punches.
"Hey!" I shout again. "What are you doing?"

"Returning the favor!" she says. "See? Getting attacked when you don't expect it really sucks, doesn't it?"

"It's not so bad," I say, and start countering her
moves. Soon, we're right where we left off last night.

She takes a step back and gets into a boxer's pose, then starts doing a little fancy footwork, à la Muhammad Ali. She comes at me with a left jab, left jab—pause— right roundhouse, quick left jab. The last left jab catches me in the mouth, but the impact gives me an extra half second where her hand is still out there. I grab her fist before she can pull it back. I use a little aikido to turn her arm at a painful angle. She bends over, going where I direct her arm, but then she kicks out with her left leg, catching me in the stomach, hard enough to make me break my grip.

We reset, both of us breathing heavy, but only just warmed up.

"How bad was it with Phantom?" she asks.

"Bad," I say, then do a couple of roundhouse kicks. She ducks under and comes into my space. When she pops up, we're chest to chest. My heart kicks into high gear. We stop. Then she pushes me back, laughing.

"He doesn't like the new you?" she asks.

"I'm not different. The outfit is."

"You're wearing the outfit when he doesn't want you to. You're different, all right."

"How was your dad?" I ask after a quick scissor kick.

Feint with the left, right elbow/block, left elbow/
block, right elbow, right elbow, left hook—block, block,
block.

"He hasn't talked to me."

"I'm sorry." Left jab, left jab, right jab, right hook.

"I'm not! Are you kidding?! I love when he leaves
me alone." Roundhouse kick. "I never understood the
whole silent treatment punishment. 'You're not talking
to me' . . . ooooo . . . big deal."

I throw a left jab that catches her in the nose. I stop
for a second. "Are you OK?" I ask.

"Please? That little tap?"

"No . . . the reason that tap connected."

Her head turns away from me. My first reaction is
to go to her, but my second reaction proves to be the
correct one. I take a step back, and just miss getting
clocked in the head with a back kick.

"My dad never stopped talking to me," she says as
she squats and spins into a low roundhouse kick. I jump
over it. "Even when he went away, we still talked."

"You mean when he went to prison?"

She rolls her eyes at me. "No, when he went to
Aruba. Yes, when he went to prison." She's annoyed, so

her jabs get a little sloppy. I bat the first couple away, then grab the last two, pull her arms across her body, and wrap her up.

"Well," she says, "somehow, I think this was your plan all along." I blush, but I don't let go. She pulls her arms in an attempt to escape, but the pulls are halfhearted . . . not even . . . more like quarter-hearted . . . more for show than an actual attempt to escape. After a couple of those, she stops even that. She takes a deep breath and leans her head forward onto my shoulder, and I'm afraid to move, because I don't want this moment to end. I don't want to be a superhero anymore. I don't want her to be my enemy. I just want to stand there . . . or wherever . . . and have Allison rest her head on my shoulder. That's it.

"Do you hear that?" she asks, looking up at me.

"Sorry," I say. "It's beating a little fast. I can't help it."

"Not that," she says, smiling. And is she blushing a little? "It sounds like . . . cheering?"

We turn our heads. Without our even realizing it, the fight took us to the edge of the building, and standing on the building directly across from us, a crowd of people has formed . . . and they're watching us . . . and cheering. One of them is holding a sign that says "Kiss!"

"How did they find us?" I ask.

"Look up, dummy."

I do. There's the news helicopter, circling overhead. "They must be doing a live feed," she says.

"Of us? But even Phantom never gets a live feed anymore." I start laughing. It doesn't seem real.

Allison starts laughing, too. "Well, we probably shouldn't waste it then. Come on. I'm sick of moping. Let's give 'em a show."

"As you wish, milady." I push her away and twirl her. There's a disappointed groan from the audience, which turns into a gasp of disbelief as Allison does an amazing set of flips, then turns to face me. She does a little of the Ali footwork, gets into her fighting stance, then gives me a little "come hither" wave . . . I laugh and get into my fighter stance, and now the crowd roars its approval and starts cheering. She starts running toward me, so I start running toward her. She leaps. I leap. We clash in midair, ten feet above the ground, throwing and countering a few punches before our momentum carries us away from each other. I roll on the ground and pop back up, just in time to see her do an awesome foot

183

slide into a one-handed handstand, twist her body, then come back down on her feet . . . back into her original fighting stance.

"Show off!" I yell.

"Jealous!" she yells back. "Come on, Bright Boy! Try to keep up!" She runs and leaps over the edge of the building. I dive after her.

She's already using her grappling hook to swing onto the roof of another building. When she lets go of the rope, she leaves the hook in place. The rope swings back up to me. It's an easy grab, but somehow, I miss. Stupid. I was too busy trying to think of a cool landing move that I took the swing for granted, and now I'm falling. The crowd gasps, but this isn't even the hardest fall I've had off a building this week. I twist into a dive. FP-154 is coming up in twenty-four seconds . . .

"You are such a klutz," Allison says, suddenly right beside me.

I smile. She came back for me. "You realize we're—"

"Falling off a building? Yeah . . . I got that."

"Uh . . . duh. No. I was going to say that we're twelve seconds from FP-154."

"FP wha—"

"Flagpole 154. Trent and I have labeled every grab-able, swingable thing on the side of every building in the city."

"Nuh-uh! That's so—"

"Amazing? Impressive?"

"Dorky."

I roll my eyes, then grab her, reach up and grab the FP-154 (right on time). I flip her up in the air. She does a quick double somersault, falls past me, and grabs the flag on the flagpole that I'm on, just to the right of me. She swings around. I drop in front of her, timed perfectly so that I can grab her legs as she comes back around. She lets go of the flag. We sail through the air. It feels like we're moving in slow-motion. I let go of her legs just before landing on the ground, feet first; she lands a split-second after. We're facing each other, three inches apart.

Allison and I look at each other in disbelief. "I've never—" she says, in between gasps for air.

"Neither have I—"

We grab each other in a hug that would break the ribs of a normal person. The crowd surrounding us on the ground erupts. The crowd peering over the edge of the building above us is going nuts. I look around in disbelief. Allison just rests her head against my chest.

"Wow," I say.

She laughs. "Which part?"

"All of it."

She lifts her head off of my chest. "How about this?" she asks, then pulls my face close to hers and kisses me. The crowd roars. At least I think they do. All I can hear is the blood rushing to my head. When she pulls away, I see the tiny lights in front of my eyes that come with any head rush . . . dancing like sparks off a bonfire.

Suddenly, there's a spotlight on us. Or maybe it was there the whole time, and we didn't notice it. "Kiss him again!" someone shouts over a bullhorn from the deck of the news chopper hovering above us. "Come on! We missed it the first time!" Allison starts laughing.

Then, suddenly, the sky explodes. It's one of Dr. Chaotic's weapons. The helicopter veers off. People scream and scatter. Allison and I look up to see Phantom Justice and Dr. Chaotic heading right toward us.

"What do we do?" I ask her. "Start fighting each other?"

She shrugs. "Maybe?"

Neither of us moves. Dr. Chaotic swoops down on

a pair of propulsion boots, grabs Monkeywrench, and zooms off. Allison looks back at me and mouths the words, *See you at school tomorrow.* I wave.

Phantom grabs my arm, midwave. "What do think you're doing?!" Phantom yells into my face.

"Waving good-bye?"

The crowd is still there watching, but now they've started to boo . . . and it's obvious I'm not the one they're unhappy with. Phantom looks at them, then looks back at me. "Come on!" he yells, then yanks my arm. After a few quick flips, we find a deserted alley. He's pacing, so fast that the asphalt under his feet is starting to heat up and get a little goopy.

"Can't . . . too many people . . . just calm," he's muttering.

"Uhh, Phantom? Trent?"

"Don't! Talk!" he says through gritted teeth. "I can't . . . not . . . yet."

I stand there and watch him as he goes through the meditation techniques he learned from a Tibetan monk or something. After a few deep breaths, he opens his eyes.

"You're suspended. Effective immediately," he says calmly.

"What? Why?"

"Why?! WHY?! WH—?!" He stops himself and goes back into meditation mode.

"Trent, liste—"

He holds up his hand to stop me, then takes a couple more deep breaths. He opens his eyes. "Go home," he says.

"OK . . . I get it . . . I shouldn't kiss our archenemy's sidekick/daughter in the middle of your big battle, but suspension? Come o—"

In a flash, he's got me by the front of my costume. He lifts me in the air. His eyes look calm, as if he and I were just having a nice conversation.

"Not yet," he says. "This no. I not. Can't."

"What?" I'm trying to make sense of what he just said, but his words seem all jumbled.

"This is not yet," he says. "Go home, or it will be."

He calmly puts me down, straightens out my shirt, then slowly backs away from me. He stands there looking at me, the same stony calmness in his eyes.

"OK," I say. "I'm going." Creeped out would be a bit of an understatement. I leap on the nearby fire escape and zip up to the roof, then skulk back to sneak a peek. Phantom is still standing there, staring at the spot I just vacated. I lie down on the roof, out of sight. I look up at the stars, and wonder if anyone in the history of the planet has ever had as bizarre a night as I've just had.

1 5

"HOW BAD WAS IT?" SHE ASKS, THEN takes a bite of her apple.

Allison finagled another "independent study" for us, so now we're sitting on the roof of the school. I have to remember to actually do all this "independent study" work . . . eventually. But for now, I'm happy just to be up here . . . with Allison . . . even if I'm not feeling all that cheerful at the moment.

"I'm on probation," I say, trying not to reveal how upset I am about it.

She starts laughing, spitting out pieces of chewed-up apple. "Probation? What does that even *mean*?"

"Super-classy with the food spitting," I say.

"I still have some left . . . see?" She opens her mouth wide to show me. "Aaaaaaahhhh."

I smile at her, but my heart's not in it.

"Seriously, though," she says, "what does he mean you're 'on probation'?"

"I guess that I can't go out as Bright Boy for a while."

"That's ridiculous!"

"He's pretty upset."

"So? Putting you 'on probation' seems a little harsh to me."

"Yeah . . . but to tell you the truth, I expected that from Phantom. It was Louis's reaction that really got to me."

"Who's Louis?"

"Technically, he's my butler . . . but really, he's the only person who's ever looked out for me." I slap my forehead in disgust. "Annnnd I probably shouldn't have given you his name."

She rolls her eyes at me. "OK, first of all . . . hellooo . . . trust issues . . . and second of all, if I *really* wanted to find where you lived, knowing the name of your butler doesn't exactly help me out."

"No, I guess not."

"I'd just follow you home one day," she says with a shrug.

I look at her suspiciously. "But you didn't."

She smiles. "No, of course not, Trusty McTrusterson," she says. "Now tell me about Louis. Is he a plus?"

"No. He's just an ex-con, ex–mixed martial arts fighter from Brooklyn. Phantom found him a couple of years before he found me. Apparently, Louis was a fight trainer at a local gym when Phantom went in for a sparring session . . . not as Phantom . . . as his alter—"

"—ego. Yeah, I got that."

"The sparring session was supposed to be a test run," I say, "to see if Phantom's training was complete. It wasn't. Louis gave him the beating of his life . . . up to that point."

"Wow. Seriously? You sure he's not a plus?" she asks.

"As sure as I can be. We've sparred a ton of times. If Louis is a plus/plus, I would've seen something."

"OK, so Louis kicked Phantom's butt, right? How?"

"Well, Louis's whole thing is that technique trumps speed and strength nine times out of ten, and his technique is amazing. The guy studies his opponents, figures out their moves and habits, and then figures out a way to take them down as quickly as possible. It's crazy."

"So Phantom hired him as what . . . A personal trainer or something?"

"Yeah, more like a personal trainer, bodyguard, caretaker kind of thing. It helps that Louis is a neat freak and an amazing cook, so he kind of covers all our bases."

I pause for a second.

"It's weird," I say. "Sometimes I kinda feel like Phantom's more concerned about how I fit into his crusade then with me personally. But Louis . . . in a lot of ways, he's my lifeline."

Allison gives me an understanding nod. I laugh.

"What?" she asks.

"Louis is a total tough guy, right? But you know what he wears around the house?"

She shakes her head.

"When I was six, I used to call him Bear, because that's what I thought he looked like the first time I saw him . . . this hairy giant who came running at me, arms wide, scooping me up off the ground and squeezing me so tight even I had trouble breathing. So, for his birthday that year, I got him a pair of teddy bear slippers."

Allison laughs. "Teddy bear slippers?"

"Yeah. They're these big, fuzzy slippers with a smiley bear face on the front of each one. I told him that I wanted his feet to get hugged like he hugs me . . . corny, I know. What do you want? I was six."

"That's not corny at all." She stops to think about it. "OK, maybe a little. So he still wears them?"

I nod. "I mean, they're a little beat-up after seven years, but he refuses to get rid of them. Imagine this big, burly guy who looks like he just stepped off a Harley, with what look like the happiest bears in the world wrapped around his feet."

She laughs. "OK, it's official . . . you need to cheer up, because there is absolutely no way a guy like that is going to stay mad at you. It's just not possible"

"No, I guess not. It just hurts knowing I disappointed him."

"He'll get over it. Trust me."

"Why, what'd your dad do?"

"Nothing, really," she says. Her legs are dangling over the side, and I swear I'm hypnotized. I could watch them all day. "He was a little weird to me this morning, but really, what's he going to do? I mean, we steal stuff. How's he going to punish me for breaking the 'rules'?"

"Aha! So, you admit you're a criminal!" I say, pointing at her.

She smiles. "Only to snap you out of your funk.

I'm not up for the whole moody-mopey thing today. In fact . . ."

"Why do I get nervous whenever you say 'in fact,' and then stop?"

"Come on," she says. She leaps off the building onto the roof next door.

"Hey!"

She turns back to me. "Sssshhh!" She gives me a wide-eyed look and points down to the street. I look over the edge and see a bunch of our classmates gathered below. The classes are over, so now kids are breaking off into their various groups: Members of sports teams start heading for practice, club members go back inside for their meetings, and a bunch of other kids just splinter off and go to Java Joe's to drink coffee and goof off. I look at Allison. She gives me an impatient "Come on!" wave. Should I even pretend that I don't want to follow her? I leap over to the next building.

She gives me a light kiss, then sprints away. I sprint right after her.

We leap across the city's rooftops . . . not speaking . . . just soaring, flipping, and turning in sync, laughing as the city supplies endless rooftops to jump from and to.

She stops suddenly, on the roof of one of the buildings

bordering the East River. I come to a sliding halt next to her. She's looking out at the Brooklyn Bridge. The sun is starting to go down, and the lights are just starting to blink on. A boat chugs lazily across the water. "I love this. This picture. Right here," she says.

"You must bring all your boyfriends up here," I say, only half-kidding.

She looks at me, a small smile on her face that tells me she knows what I was fishing for. "What makes you think you're my boyfriend?"

And I have one of those moments where, even after everything that's happened, I don't know if she's kidding or not. And then she takes my hand and smiles at me. "I mean, you are . . . if you want to be," she says. "But what makes you think that you are?"

"You may not know this about me, but I am a world-famous detective and crime fighter."

"Nooo!"

"Yes! And I could tell how you felt about me the moment we met! Five years ago! When I thought you were a boy . . . wait . . ."

She laughs and slaps me "lightly" on the shoulder.

"I don't think you know how hard you slap," I say.

"Ohhh, poor super-strong baby," she says. Then she

grabs my arm and puts it around her shoulders. We stand there and watch the world get darker and the lights on the bridge get brighter.

"May I ask you something?" she says.

"Sure."

"Did you ever think that this was all a setup?"

"Puh-leeze. The only reason I'd think this was a setup was if I had *any* doubts about my"—pause—"irresistibility." I give her a wink, followed by my cheesiest grin.

"So, you thought it was a setup, then."

"Oh, yeah. Definitely."

She tilts her head up and kisses me. "Wow," I say. "What'll you do if I tell you I thought you were going to kill me?" I ask.

She smiles. "You're being honest with me. You could've lied and said no, just so I wouldn't let go."

"How would you have known it was a lie?"

"Well, probably because I'm not an idiot. We're archenemies. If you weren't suspicious of me, even a little bit, you're either lying or stupid."

"So . . . were you suspicious of me, then?"

"What do you mean *were*? Try 'still am.'" She laughs.

"Are you?"

She's not laughing anymore. "Look, if I want to be completely honest, I started 'being friends' with you because I thought I could find new and interesting ways to kick the snot out of you."

"Yeah. Me, too." I pause. "So how are we ever going to totally trust each other?"

Allison looks at me. "Is there ever such a thing as two people *totally* trusting each other?"

Before I can answer, she kisses me. And suddenly I am not so worried about trust anymore.

"AAAAAAAAAAAAAA!!!!!!!!!!!!!!"

A piercing scream startles us apart.

"What the heck was that?" Allison says.

The selfish side of me doesn't want to answer. But I know what it is . . . I've heard it hundreds of times . . . and I can't ignore it. "It's a scream for help," I say. "Wait here."

She laughs at me. "Yeah, right! Come on . . . which way?"

"AAAAAAAA!!!!"

I listen to the sound, triangulating the direction from the way it's bouncing off the buildings. I point to the right corner of the roof. "This way."

We sprint toward the sound. One more scream, so I know where you are . . . come on.

"AAAAAAA!!!!! Stop!!! STOP!!!!"

"Come on!" I yell to Allison.

Three rooftops away, we see them. A woman is on the ground, cradling the bleeding head of an unconscious man. They're dressed like bikers. Six guys, all in nice khakis and dress shirts, have formed a circle around them; one of them is holding a tire iron and looks like he knows how to use it. The woman on the ground is crying. The six guys are laughing.

Allison looks concerned but confused. "What do we do?" she asks. "We need masks."

"No time. Relax . . . wait . . . follow my lead," I tell her.

The woman on the ground is sobbing. "Please . . . he's hurt . . . please . . . ." From where I'm standing, the guy's wound looks superficial. On the other hand, he is unconscious . . . and there's nothing superficial about the tire iron that threatening guy is holding.

He's about six feet three inches tall, two hundred twenty pounds, athletic, black belt in at least one martial art, possibly two, looks like he's had a couple of drinks, but not drunk enough to be impaired . . . just enough to make him think he's invincible.

"He's my husband! Please!"

"All I wanted to do was talk to you," the guy with the tire iron growls. "Talking time's over now." He's moving toward the unconscious guy, raising the tire iron, about to strike.

I step in front of him. He stops short. "What the . . . ?"

"Nice night, isn't it, gentlemen?" I say.

"Get out of my way, kid," he says. The tire iron is still raised in the go position.

"OK . . . here's the thing, Captain Dress Pants," I say, "you're going to put the tire iron down and wait nicely for the police to arrive, or we're going to play a little game . . . it's called Let's See How Far I Can Cram That Tire Iron Down Your Throat. Doesn't that sound fun?"

He hesitates . . . sizes me up . . . and starts laughing. His friends laugh with him, and I can't help thinking that I'm looking at Jake Berkshire's not-too-distant future. "You gotta be kidding me?"

"Put the tire iron down."

"Kid, you just wrote a check you can't cash."

"You heard him," Allison says, stepping out of the shadows. "Surrender! To justice!"

Silence. I snicker. I try to hold it in, but it's no use. "Surrender to justice?"

"What? I've never done this before."

"Yeah . . . no kidding."

"Hey!" Captain Dress Pants yells, all slurry. "What's goin' on here?"

"Oh well, that's easy," Allison says, "You and your idiot friends are about to win an all-expenses-paid trip to the hospital of your choice."

"You better watch it, honey . . . or after I smash up your boyfriend here, you'll be next. Hate to mess up that pretty face of yours," he says while laughing.

I'm about to break his neck when Allison holds her hand up to me. She smiles slyly. "Ooooo . . . such tough talk! How tough do you think your talk's going to be after this pretty-faced little honey humiliates you in front of your friends? Hm?"

Captain Dress Pants's friends all cry "OHHHH!" The laughter is now directed at him, and he doesn't like it one bit. "Listen," he snarls, "I don't care if you are a little girl. I'm going to rip your little head off your little neck."

Allison starts laughing, then turns to me. "What do you think, tae kwon do?" she asks, then gets into a tae kwon do pose. "Ooo! Or how about hapkido?" She shifts her stance.

"You know, I don't think he deserves a fight pose," I say.

"You know, I think you're right," Allison says.

Allison and I just stand there with our arms crossed, not moving. Captain Dress Pants looks at us funny, as if he has a moment of awareness . . . as if something in the back of his Cro-Magnon brain is alerting him that maybe he's misread the situation, and that maybe this isn't such a good idea. Just as I think he's about to make some lame excuse and put the crowbar down, he does the stupid thing and charges.

I have to hand it to him . . . for a guy who isn't plus/plus, his charge isn't half-bad. Unfortunately for him, it isn't half-good, either. He leads with the crowbar (of course), swinging it directly at my head. I put my hand up and catch the crowbar. I hold on to it, pivot in my crouch, then snap the bar forward. The guy goes flying. I'm holding the crowbar. The guy has some training, because he somersaults up and is ready to go again. Any doubts he might have had are gone now; he's in attack mode. He comes sprinting back at me.

"Do you want him?" I ask Allison.

"Shouldn't you, as my boyfriend, be defending me?"

"Uh, he's almost here," I say.

"Answer the question."

"Do you want him or not?"

"Answer the question."

"Do . . . you . . . want . . . him . . . or . . . not?" I ask, enunciating each word.

She smiles wide. "Of course, I want him. Just testing to see if you were 'that' kind of guy."

"Nope. I'm not. He's all yours."

"You always know just what to get me," she says.

I slide out of the path of the charging idiot. She slides into the space I just left, sidesteps his clumsy punch, and with just her thumb and forefinger grabs his wrist and pulls it down in an arc underneath him. With his momentum, he flips completely over onto his back. He immediately flicks himself back up with one of those kung-fu moves that looks so impressive when you're eight years old.

"Oooo," Allison purrs. "You've got a little fight in you. Let's see how much."

Although it is a lot of fun to watch Alison work (it must be . . . Captain Dress Pants's friends haven't moved yet . . . they're all just standing around, stunned), I realize I should probably check in on the victims.

"Are you OK?" I ask the woman and the man who is now just coming to.

"Yeah," he says. He's groggy and his pupils are dilated.

"They were bothering me," the woman says. "Sean told them to leave us alone. They did but then waited until we got out here and jumped us." Her breathing is shallow. She's trying not to cry. "They hit Sean from behind with the tire iron."

"It's all right now," I say. "As soon as we're done here, I'll call an ambulance."

"Is that a girl fighting him?" Sean says.

"You have a minor concussion, sir," I say, "but yes, that is a girl fighting him, and no, you're not imagining this."

"Who are you?" the woman asks.

"No one," I say, smiling. "Hey, A.M.!" I yell.

"Yeah?" she says.

"You just about finished with Captain Dress Pants?"

"Yeah, I think so. You're not getting tired on me, are you, big boy?" She gives him a casual pat on the face. He tries to knock her head off. She ducks and laughs. "Yup. Almost done."

"Great!" I say. Captain Dress Pants's idiot friends have finally realized that their buddy might not win the fight.

They turn to me.

"Hey! Kid! You're dead meat!"

"Pff . . . OK," I laugh. "Let's party."

"Dead meat!!"

They all let out a yell and start to rush me. I get into my fighting stance, and am about to kick into one of my more impressive moves (if I do say so myself) when all of a sudden, Captain Dress Pants comes flying in like a wrecking ball (back-first) and knocks his friends flat. They fall face-first into the pavement. *Whap! Whap! Whap!*

"Hey!" I say.

"What?" Allison says as she comes walking over. "Oh, look . . . perfect strike."

"Did you throw your opponent into my opponents?"

"Uhh . . . yeah. I thought that was obvious."

"I was . . . I had a . . . I was just about to take care of this."

"Well, now you don't have to."

"That's not the point. I . . ." I exhale. "I wanted to impress you, OK?"

"Oh, but you did! You were fantas—oh, look who's up again."

Captain Dress Pants is now slowly trying to stand back

up, as if he's not quite sure what happened, but he . . . has . . . to . . . keep . . . fighting!

"That's beautiful," I say, then tap my chest twice. "He has a warrior's heart."

Just as he moves his fists up to a fighting stance, Allison zips over and punches him out. *Wham!* And down he goes.

"And a ballet dancer's jaw," Allison says. "Jeez!"

"Wha—" I sputter. "You could've at *least* let me do THAT one."

"Oh, I'm sorry!" she says, then looks at me disapprovingly. "Looks like someone needs to be a little quicker on the draw."

"Won't even let me pretend to protect her . . ." I mutter.

She gives me a big kiss on the cheek. "I thought you were *very* impressive. Dashing, even."

"Thank you," I say begrudgingly. "But I didn't get to hit anybody."

"Next time. Deal?"

"Deal."

Just then, we start to hear the sirens approaching from several blocks away.

"Well," I say, "there's our cue. Sean, take care of that noggin, buddy, OK?" Sean and his wife nod as if they're certain they're dreaming this.

"Gentlemen," Allison says, "it's been a pleasure . . . kind of . . . not really . . . but whatever . . . Say good night, Scotty."

"Good night, Scotty," I say.

And with that, we bow our heads, tip invisible hats, and then slip off into the shadows.

16

IT'S NIGHT SO. OF COURSE. THE ALLEY is dark . . . but this is more of a "no light can escape" dark than a "it's kind of hard to see" dark. It's the kind of alley where a body might lie for a couple of days before anyone finds it. The guy standing in the alley isn't worried about this. Why should he be? He's huge. Six feet five inches, more than three hundred pounds of solid muscle. He's the kind of guy who makes dead bodies in random alleys, not becomes one.

The name he's using at the moment is Justin Wheeler, but sometimes he goes by another one: Rogue Warrior. He checks his watch again. He's early.

"You're early," says a voice from the darkness behind him.

"So are you," Justin replies.

"I guess so," says the voice. Trent Clancy steps out of the shadows.

Justin smiles. "Whew . . . for a minute, I thought you were going to be in costume, and that I forgot to wear mine or something."

Trent laughs. "Nope . . . just a casual meeting."

Justin laughs in relief. "Oh, before I forget, thanks for what you did to the witness."

"Yes, well after her 'ordeal,' I thought she could use a trip to Aruba. Too bad she missed the inquest."

"Yeah. Thanks!"

"That's OK. I mean, all you did was waste three months of planning by taking a random bank teller hostage instead of a celebrity, like we talked about."

"I couldn't . . . They're kinda hard to fi—"

"Then, to really screw it up, you chose a roof that was *eighty* stories high, instead of eight, so that no one could hear your demands."

Justin looks worried. "Sorry."

"It's OK. Really. We're all in this together, right?" Trent says with a reassuring smile. "I just had to get those last, little passive-aggressive bits out, you know?"

Justin smiles back.

"So you said you had something you need help on," Justin says. "Is it another gig?"

"Not quite. No. I mean it's no big deal, but you did screw up your last job, right?"

Justin looks at his shoes. "Yeah."

"So, I think it may be a while before you get another one."

"No! I'll do better next time! I swear!" Justin's eyes get a little moist with tears. His breathing is uneven.

"Stop," Trent says in a soothing voice. "It's OK. It's only for a little while. Plus, there are lots of things you can do to still be helpful."

"Anything! I'll do anything!"

"Good to know," Trent says, "because there's actually something you can do right now."

"Oh yeah? What?"

"Stand still," Trent says, and pulls out a dart gun. It makes a small *foop* sound when it fires. The dart is tiny and looks absolutely ridiculous in Justin's enormous neck.

"Wha—" is all Justin is able to say before the convulsions start. His right hand clutches his chest over his heart.

"Chaotic and I have been working on it. Well, that's not entirely true. Chaotic has been the one working on it. I'm just the lucky guy who gets to test it."

"H-h-h-h . . . h-h-h-h . . ." Justin is wheezing now, clutching his chest harder.

"Funny you should ask," Trent says. "It's a special formula, designed for a plus/plus, speed and strength, such as yourself. You see, our bodies are different than normal people's. Sure, we have speed and strength. And our bodies have adapted to allow for this . . . muscles, tendons, and such are all stronger, because they have to be."

"H-h-h-help . . . h-h-h-h . . ." Justin wheezes.

"And the heart . . . well, the heart is just another muscle . . . and our special abilities put quite a strain on the ol' ticker." Trent taps his chest for emphasis. "Luckily, our hearts have adapted to that . . . somewhat. I mean, they're still not fully up to the job our bodies give them. In fact, I can't help but think of all the plus/plus souls who died young because they had no idea, and just pushed their poor little hearts too far." Trent bows his head in mourning. It almost looks sincere.

Justin's wheezes are getting further apart . . . more strained. He falls on his back.

"And that's why all it takes is a strong shot of specialized adrenaline into the bloodstream, and BOOM! You go into cardiac arrest. Just . . . like . . . so . . ."

"H-h-h-h-help . . ."

"You are helping, Justin. A great deal, in fact. Probably in the only way a big, clumsy ox like yourself can help . . . by becoming a test case. A big, steroid-filled lab rat. Now we know it works . . . and when the time comes when we have to . . . tie up a couple of loose ends, well—"

Trent looks down at Justin, lying on his back in the dark and filthy alley. The big man's eyes are bulging out of his head. His wheezing is getting fainter and fainter. Trent holds Justin's wrist, monitoring his pulse. It weakens . . . slows . . . stops completely. The wheezing has stopped as well. Trent holds on for a minute longer, to see if his pulse comes back, but it doesn't. The dart in his neck has now completely dissolved, leaving nothing but a minuscule red dot. It's smaller than a mosquito bite, less noticeable than a shaving nick. If you weren't looking for it, you'd never notice it.

"Thank you for your service, Rogue Warrior. You will be forgotten." Trent smiles, drops the big arm, and walks casually out of the alley. For some reason, he feels like whistling, so he does.

"Well?" Edward asks without turning around. "Did it work?"

"I really can't sneak up on you, can I?" Trent says, stepping out of the lab's shadows.

"No. But I fully expect you to keep trying. Eventually, I may lie to you, just so you can claim victory and stop trying."

"And I may let you, just so I can claim victory and stop trying."

"So, did it work?" Edward asks again.

"Perfectly."

"I told you it would."

"You tell me lots of things, but they're not always true. Do I have to remind you about that laser version of this?"

"The laser worked . . . maybe not exactly the way we planned it, but it worked."

"Yes, well the dart may not be as cool as a laser, but it works much better."

"And the antidote?" Edward asks.

"Whoops!" Trent says in mock surprise. "You know, I totally forgot to give him that."

"What?!" Edward is up in a flash. "You killed him?"

"Killed him? Killed who? I have no idea what you're

talking about! I met up with a guy who suddenly went into cardiac arrest, and well . . . what can I say . . . I guess I just panicked."

"You murdered him."

"He was a complete screwup."

"That means he deserved to die?" Edward asks.

"No. He deserved to be a test subject, because he proved that he couldn't do anything else well. Unfortunately for him, the test proved to be fatal."

"That's quite a justification."

"And that's quite a conscience you're growing there, Doc. I'm not sure I like what I'm hearing."

"What are you hearing?" Edward asks.

"I'm hearing a guy who might decide not to do what he needs to do. I'm hearing a guy who might hang me out to dry."

"You can trust me."

"Can I really? Because here you are, getting all bent out of shape over Rogue Warrior, a big, dumb screwup that you barely knew. What are you going to say if we need to use this on your 'daughter'? Huh?"

"Nothing. I'll say nothing"

"Really? Why do I find that so hard to believe?"

"I don't know. Why do you? Maybe it's because you

don't want to acknowledge the REAL problem I have with what you just did, because it makes you look like an idiot! You just made a *body* . . . and that *body* can be studied, and if a smart enough investigator is the one doing the studying, they might be able to trace it back to us."

"Nobody's going to be able to trace it back to us."

"How do you know?" Edward yells at him. "There *are* other plus intelligences out there, you know! Look, you just made a loose end. And that loose end can lead to others."

Trent starts laughing. "You're so dramatic! Do you know how many loose ends there are on a daily basis in a city this big? Hm? Trust me. I speak from experience."

"Experience as a witness . . . or experience as someone who makes loose ends?"

Trent smiles. "Well, let's just say I like to dabble. *Lots* of murders go unsolved in this city ."

"It was risky . . . and pointless . . . that's all."

"You're wrong, Doc. It was neither. We needed to know if the dart penetrated the skin, and whether it would dissolve without leaving a trace . . . but we also needed to know if it would put our targets down permanently, or just for a little while. And now we know."

"Yes . . . great . . . and maybe the police will know, too."

"There's no way . . . and even if there was, so what?"

"You're not the one who'll be up for murder charges!" Edward yells.

"And neither will you, if you stay calm and stick to the plan," Trent says. "What is your problem?"

"Nothing."

"Was I wrong about you?" Trent asks. His mouth is curled in an ugly sneer. "You're trying to get out of it, aren't you? You actually *feel* something for your little sidekick? I thought your cold, calculating plus intellect had kicked in. I thought she was just a pawn to you."

"She is."

"Why don't I believe you?"

"I don't know, Trent. Maybe because you don't want to," Edward says.

"And what is that supposed to mean?"

"I've heard rumors, too . . . about strength and speed pluses like you . . . about the possible side effects of that little 'gift' as you get older . . . about why right now you might be a little desperate. This all might be coming to an en—"

Trent places his hand over Edward's mouth.

"Sssshhhh," he says, moving in until he and Edward are nose-to-nose. "You don't want to say that," he whispers. "That'll just hurt my feelings."

Trent's eyes look black . . . opaque . . . drained of any significant human emotion. Edward tries not to shiver, but a little one sneaks out.

"Listen, Edward," Trent says, his voice lowering to a tone that sounds almost sane, "I know this is going to be a bit of a change, and you're not all that thrilled about change, in any form . . . but what choice do we have? IGO is getting restless. You know, they threatened to pull out of the deal?"

"When?"

"This morning. They're upset, Edward. They put millions on the table, and they want us to deliver, and if we don't, well . . . they mentioned that they might have to do something drastic. Now, I can't say I blame them . . . they spent a lot of money, and they want results, and well, we're just not getting them. And why aren't we getting them, Edward?"

Edward doesn't say anything.

"That's right," Trent continues, "Because we've managed to lose the key young demographic. And why do you think that is? Hm? Because it's been stolen from us, by our sidekicks. The stupid public and their stupid love of stupid romance. 'Ohhhh, they're on different sides of the law!' 'Ohhh, it's just so ro-freakin'-mantic!' Morons." His face breaks into an easy, relaxed smile. "But what can you do, right? The public wants what it wants, right? And you know what's even more romantic than two little tweety birds from opposite sides of the tracks falling in love? Two little tweety birds from opposite sides of the tracks falling in love and dying.

"All the screaming little girls and boys who can't wait to see them kiss and hug and all that junk will cry themselves to sleep at night at the thought of Monkeywrench and Bright Boy loving each other in the afterlife," Trent continues. "And all of them will tune in to our final battle, as the two mourning father figures fight each other for revenge."

"Final battle? Are you going to kill me, too?"

"Only if you step out of line," Trent says, then laughs. "Kidding! I'm kidding! What good would it do to kill the golden goose? You realize, once we set this thing in motion, all of our battles from here on out will be huge! We'll always be battling over our fallen children. And that will always suck in a new audience, looking for teen love and tragic romance. The kids will be dead, but their

story . . . their passion . . . will live on, forever . . . sniff .
. . sob . . ." Trent laughs. "And you and I will rake it in."

"Sounds good," Edward says.

"Of course, it sounds good. You'd have to be deaf for
it not to sound good. Well, Edward . . . are you deaf?"

"Just stop, OK. Maybe I'm not as ecstatic about
killing a couple of teenagers as you seem to be, but I'd
have to be an idiot to not see the possibilities. And—"

"You're not an idiot," Trent says. "Exactly. Two little
pawns taken off the board, and you and I are set for life."

"Sounds good. When?"

Trent smiles. "No time like the present."

17

"ARE YOU OK?" I ASK. WE'VE BEEN
on Allison's favorite roof, looking out at the Brooklyn Bridge for the past half hour, and she's been quiet the whole time.

"Yeah. I'm fine," she says in a way that is clearly not fine.

"Did I do something wrong?"

"You? Oh God, no . . ."

"So there is something wrong, it just isn't my fault."

She sighs. "You can be a real pain sometimes, you know that?"

"OK, so *now* it's my fault?"

That gets a smile out of her, but then her eyes start tearing up. She puts a hand over them to try to hide it, and I know enough about her to know that she's not thrilled with the idea of crying in front of someone . . . anyone.

"Allison?"

"It's nothing," she says in the slurry way people talk when they're talking and crying at the same time.

"Right. It's nothing. Obviously."

"I feel like an idiot, OK?" she says, and the tears are really coming now.

"What? Why?"

She wipes her eyes, but the tears keep falling.

"Tonight, when that woman screamed and you stopped kissing me, there was a little voice in the back of my head that was like, Only a dork stops kissing a girl in order to go save someone he doesn't even know. How horrible is that?"

"Absolutely horrible. So horrible, in fact, that I was thinking the EXACT SAME THING. You think I wanted to go save someone instead of kissing you?"

"No! And that's my point! You didn't want to go, but you did! Because you knew someone was in trouble! I would never do that."

"What are you talking about?! You went with me, remember?"

"Yeah . . . tonight. But how many nights in the past five years have you done this? Huh?"

I thought about it. There were too many to count.

"Too many to count, right?" she said. "And how many times have I done it? Counting tonight . . . once."

"So?"

She sniffles, takes a deep breath, and lets it out quickly. "So, all this time—even these past couple of days—I thought you were naive. . . . I thought you'd have to be to be a 'good guy.' Saving the world, one person at a time . . . and while you're helping other people—people you don't even know—your own life is going right down the toilet."

"That seems a little harsh, but OK . . ."

"I thought only a total sap would do that."

I shrug. I don't know what to say.

"Except I was wrong," she says. "Look at you. You don't even know what to say right now because you're trying not to hurt my feelings. You're trying not to point out the obvious . . . except it wasn't obvious to someone selfish like me. You're not trying to save the world . . . you're trying to save the people in it. You're not naive . . . You're noble." She's crying hard now. "And I'm a jerk."

I start laughing. I can't help it. "Bull," I say. "And

I'm not just saying that because I want you to stop crying so we can get back to the making-out portion of the evening. Although, if you wanted to stop right now so we can get back to making out, I wouldn't think less of you."

She laughs through her tears, but then immediately goes back to crying.

"You wanted a normal life," I say. "There's nothing selfish about that."

"Yes, there is. When you're like us, it's completely selfish to pretend like you can't help people because you want to fit in . . . because you want to have friends, and go out, and have fun."

I shake my head and am about to argue, but she cuts me off.

"Five years!" she says. "Do you know how many people I could have helped in five years?"

"No. I don't. And neither do you. So stop beating yourself up over it. All I know is that when I went to go help those people tonight, you were right beside me . . . And quite frankly, that's how I'd like things to be from now on."

She nods, but in a distracted way, as if she's only half-listening to me. I take her in my arms and hold her. She lets me. Her tears are winding down. She wipes her face on my shirt, then looks up at me. I'm about to kiss her when she pulls away from me

"Oh man," she says, taking her phone out of her pocket. "My dad just texted me."

She opens her phone to read it when my phone goes off. It's Trent. For a second, I consider not answering it. I don't really want to talk to him. Plus, I'm suspended, right? That means he doesn't get to call me.

The phone rings again. I pick it up.

"Scott?"

"Yeah."

"It's Trent. Listen"—he pauses—"I think I was a little harsh on you last night . . . no . . . wait . . . I don't think . . . I KNOW I was a little harsh on you."

"Oh . . . uh . . . OK . . ."

"I'm sorry. I'm just"—he takes a deep breath, then lets it out—"I'm just a little frustrated. You know how important justice is to me."

I don't know what the proper response to that is, so I just say, "Uh-huh."

"And well, it's just killing me that filth like Dr. Chaotic is running loose in the city. I just wanted to make sure that it was killing you, too," he says.

"Trent, listen. I'm still with you. I am. I just needed to make a few changes, that's all."

"No, I get it. I get it. You're getting older now, and . . . well, you're going to start having your own opinions"— he stops—"no. Wait. Scratch that. You've had your own opinions for a while, it's just that now you're a little more forward in voicing them, right?"

"Right," I say cautiously.

"And I'm not really used to that . . . and I didn't really handle it as well as I could have. In fact, I didn't handle it well at all."

"No, you didn't," I say. I look over at Allison, but she's still hunched over her phone, tapping away.

"I have no excuse. You've saved my life, for God's sake. The least I could do is show you the respect you've earned many times over. I'm sorry," he says . . . and is that a sniffle? "Hold on a second." He puts the phone down, and I hear it again. It's definitely a sniffle.

I'm too shocked to say anything. Trent has never expressed anything close to this to me before, let alone gotten all teary. I mean, I knew he cared, I guess I just never realized how much.

I look over at Allison. She waves to me, then points and mouths the words *I have to go*. Her eyes look worried.

I want go over to her, but I don't want Trent to hear that I'm with Allison, not when it seems like he's starting to trust me again. I give her an "Are you OK?" look. She nods yes and gives me a small smile. I give her a "Really?" look; she mouths the words *I have to go* again. I mouth *OK* back to her. She smiles, a genuine one this time (but still with a small trace of worry in it), then turns and leaps off into the night.

"Scott?" It's Trent. He's back. "Sorry about that."

"It's OK."

"You have to understand that this is all new to me," he continues. "I"—he stops, takes another deep breath —"I don't always know what I'm doing. I never had a mentor, and well, I guess I let the power go to my head. I've been trying to be an example for you, lead you . . . but I guess you're older now, and you're going to have your own ideas about things."

"You don't sound happy about it."

"The only thing I'm not happy about," he says, "is how I've handled things so far. And the frustrating thing is I went through what you're going through . . . exactly! I mean, I was the kid in school who had a big secret and had a hard time connecting with people because of it."

"Really?"

"Of course. I mean, I didn't have a secret identity then, but I knew there was something different about me, and I did everything in my power to hide it. Part of me wanted everyone to know the amazing things that I was capable of, but I had a feeling that it wouldn't go over too well. I was afraid people would think I was a freak. I was afraid that whatever I accomplished would be taken away from me, and I would lose my temper and do something I regretted."

"You've never told me this."

"Yes, well . . . I guess I always thought of you as a little kid. I kind of missed the point when you grew up"—he pauses—"but things are going to be different from now on. Very, very different."

227

"Thanks, Trent. This really means a lot to me."

"Not as much as it means to—wait . . . hold on . . . the perimeter alarm is going off."

I can hear the alarm going off in the background. Suddenly, there's an explosion.

"What was that?" I yell. My mind feels like it's running in thirty different directions at once. I don't know what to do

"Dr. Chaotic!" Trent yells. "He's here! He's— Aaaaa!" There's another explosion, this one closer to Trent.

I hear the phone clatter to the ground.

"No!" I shout. "Trent! Trent!"

The only response I get is another series of explosions that almost blows out the speaker in my phone. I'm about to race home when Dr. Chaotic picks up the phone.

"Bright Boy, I presume. Or should I call you Scott? You had a lovely home here, Scott! Ha-ha-ha-ha!" A jumble of images flash across my mind: a giant hole in the wall of Trent's study with the wallpaper still smoldering around the edges, the leather couch split in half and coughing up its stuffing, papers and debris scattered all around the room. Dr. Chaotic is using telepathy to show me his handiwork.

"How did you—?" I start to ask.

"How do you think? You didn't actually believe she liked you, did you?" Dr. Chaotic starts laughing, then stops short. "Whoops! I guess you did! Awww . . . such a poor, naive, lovestruck little sidekick. So I guess you also believed her when she told you that she *didn't* follow you home! Oh, Bright Boy! So trusting! But I guess that's what makes you . . . noble!" He busts out laughing again.

The back of my head tingles as if someone just hit me with a two-by-four. I can feel the heat rising to my cheeks, out of fury and shame, anger and embarrassment. "Where's Phantom?"

"Oh, don't worry. I haven't killed him . . . yet." An image of Trent lying unconscious on the ground, covered in debris, flashes through my mind. Then another image replaces it . . . an image that knocks the wind out of me. My stomach cramps up, doubling me over. "Looks like this guy wasn't so lucky, though!" cackles Chaotic.

"It's a lie," I say. "This whole thing. It's not real."

"What's wrong, Bright Boy? Can't face the fact that your big, cuddly bear is dead? Hm? Maybe a picture will help!"

My phone dings. I have a new message . . . a photo message. I open it. It's a photo of the same image that Chaotic mentally sent to me: it's a charred corpse wearing the still-smoking remains of jeans, a shirt I gave Louis for Christmas last year…and the bear slippers. There's no mistaking them. They're smiling happily at me. One of them is missing an eye.

"Louis . . ." I whisper. My eyes sting as tears start to form. "This isn't real. It's not real."

"As real as the tears on your face, kid," Chaotic says. "You could race home and see for yourself, but if you do, you won't have the time to save your partner! And really, what's the rush? This guy's not going anywhere!"

I take a deep breath. "I'm going to kill you, Chaotic." I say, feeling strangely calm. "Do you hear me?"

"Oh, I hear you, Scotty Boy . . . believe me, I hear you. And you know what? I'm going to give you your shot. It's only fair. Ha! Plus, I want this over with, once and for all. I'm too smart to underestimate you, and I don't want to spend the rest of my life looking over my shoulder. So . . . here's the deal: I'm going to take Sleepy here back to that warehouse we were at the other night. You remember that warehouse?"

I nod, even as the image of the warehouse and the address pop into my head.

"Good boy! The whole family will be there, waiting for you! And you'll get your shot. You have fifteen minutes to get there. After that, I start removing limbs. His, not mine . . . but I suppose you probably guessed that. Ha!! See you there! Oh, and wear your costume. I want this to look official!"

Chaotic hangs up on me. I stare at the bear slippers in the picture on my phone. I don't want to look at them anymore, but I can't stop staring. It's my fault. Louis is dead and it's all my fault. I stare at the slippers a little bit longer . . . as penance.

"I'm sorry, Louis. I know it's not good enough, but I'm sorry." I check the clock on my phone. Two minutes have passed. I have thirteen to get to the warehouse. Thirteen minutes before I can start tearing into Dr. Chaotic . . . and his daughter.

I don't even want to think her name.

I start moving.

18

I GET TO THE WAREHOUSE ON ROW

Street. I still have a minute and a half, even after the stop at one of my costume stashes. So I do a quick visual sweep, even though I know it's useless. Chaotic is too good to plant his booby traps in plain sight.

I check my clock. It's time.

I burst through the roof of the warehouse.

Allison turns. "Scott?" She looks shocked to see me, but I can't tell if her shock is fake or sincere. Dr. Chaotic doesn't look surprised at all.

"Where is he?" I scream.

"Where's who?!" Allison says. "Scott, what are you—?"

"Shut up, Allison!" I yell at her, then look at her father. "WHERE IS HE?"

Allison turns to her father. "What did you do?" she yells at him. Then she turns to me. "Scott! What happened? Tell me what happened?"

"You know what happened!" I yell. "You killed Louis and kidnapped Trent! Now where is he?"

"What?! No, I didn't!"

Suddenly, there's the harsh squeal of tearing metal from right outside the warehouse. The warehouse wall starts to bend, buckle, then finally get peeled back. Trent jumps through the hole in the wall. "Chaotic! You should have known that cage wouldn't hold me!"

Allison comes over to me. She grabs my shoulders. "Scott!" Allison says. "Scott! I didn't know he was here! Honest!"

"She's lying, Scott!" Trent yells. "I heard them talking! This is a game they're playing! They're trying to confuse you!"

"No, I'm not!" Allison yells. "I DON'T KNOW WHAT'S GOING ON!"

"Louis is dead, Scott! He's dead! And it's all their fault!" Trent yells. "They did it together!"

"No!" Allison shouts.

"It was both of th— AAAAA!" Dr. Chaotic hits Trent with some kind of weapon that sends him flying backward. Chaotic goes after him. Trent hits him. Chaotic is able to dodge, but his weapon fires again, this time knocking Allison and me through the wall. We land on the ground outside. I push myself off her, flipping back onto my feet. I advance on her, swinging a right hook. She ducks.

"Scott!" she yells. "Scott!"

I swing again. She ducks again. "Your father told me, Allison!"

"What, Scott? What did he tell you?"

"You lied to me!" Kick.

"No!"

"You used me!" Jab.

"Scott, no!"

Jab. Knee. She avoids my blows, but she's not fighting back.

"Are you happy? Huh? I told you about Louis, the one person in the world who cared about me, and then he killed him!" I throw another punch, and another, and another. She dodges them all. "Did you get a good laugh out of it?"

"I didn't tell him about Louis!"

"Don't lie to me!"

"I'm not lying!" she yells at me.

"You're a villain! You've always been a villain! And now you want me to believe that you wouldn't lie to me? That you wouldn't manipulate me?"

"I told you! I was at first! But I stopped!"

"Liar!" I scream, and punch again. The tears in my eyes are making her blurry. "You're a liar!"

"NO! I'm NOT, DAMN IT!" she screams back at me. She's crying, too. "I'll turn myself in! Is that what you want?!"

"I don't know what I want!"

I throw a punch, but she just stands there. She doesn't even try to stop it or get out of the way. I pull the punch at the last second. I look at her. She's standing there, not moving, stubborn and defiant.

"Tell me you didn't tell him!" I yell.

"I didn't tell him," she says.

"Tell me you'll give all this up for me!"

"Everything. Right now. I'm done with everything." She steps toward me, close enough to kiss. She looks up at me. Tears are streaming down her face. "I didn't betray you, Scott. I couldn't, even if my dad wanted me to."

I'm breathing hard. I'm still crying. Her eyes are

locked onto mine. She puts her hands on the sides of my face. "I couldn't," she says.

I open my mouth, not sure what's going to come out. "I—"

The wall to the warehouse blows out. The blast sends us flying.

"Don't touch her!" Dr. Chaotic yells. He's pointing a weapon at me. It looks like a little dart gun. He fires. I'm about to dive out of the dart's path when someone pushes me from behind. I fall; the dart flies over me and hits Allison in the neck.

She immediately pulls it out. It starts to dissolve in her hand. She looks at me. "Scott," she says before the convulsions start. She falls to the ground.

"Allison!" I scream. "Allison!"

I race to her. She's clutching at her chest, above her heart. She's wheezing. She can't breathe. I'm sitting over her. I don't know what to do!

"ALLISON!" I scream in her face. I start looking around frantically. "We have to help her! We have to— WHAT DID YOU DO TO HER?!"

"Sorry, kid," Trent says, standing over us. He's pointing the dart gun at me. "End of the line. I'm just glad I get to do the honors."

"Wha—?" My mind is racing. "WHAT IS GOING ON?!" Allison is clawing at my arm.

Before I can do anything else, Trent fires. I'm too confused to get out of the way. The dart hits me in the neck.

"Wh—?" Before I can say another word, my heart starts racing. Suddenly, I can't breathe. I feel like someone dropped a truck on my chest. My heart feels like it's going to explode. I fall to my knees and collapse next to Allison. She looks at me. She's scared.

"Why?" Trent asks. His voice is muted . . . distorted . . . like he's underwater. "Well, lots of reasons . . . but I don't feel like going into them right now. I mean, what's the point?"

Allison's breath is getting shallower. Her grip is getting weaker . . . I have to—

"Let's just say I've been waiting for this moment for a long time," Trent says.

I'm trying to shake it off . . . stand up . . . but I can't even breathe. My chest is full of lead weights.

Trent looks down at us. "Isn't this sweet? Young love. Dying together . . . if only you didn't completely lose all faith and trust in her a couple of minutes ago, huh? I bet even if you both survived, it'll be hard to get past that, right? But as it stands, you only have a couple of more minutes to worry about it."

I look over at Allison. She grabs my hand. Hers is cold and clammy.

"Oh no," Trent says, lifting me off the ground with one hand. "We'll have none of that 'unspoken forgiveness.' Not here. You guys can sort that all out in the afterlife. Here . . . I'll give you a head start!" he shouts, then punches me. Hard. I lose my grip on Allison's hand. I'm disoriented . . . where am I going? I feel weightless as I fly through the air. I crash into something metal. I stop flying and start falling. When I land, the ground knocks what little air I have left out of me. I taste blood. I can't breathe. Blackness is creeping in.

I try to pick myself up, but I no longer know where up is.

Allison. I have to get to Allison. She wasn't lying. I have to get to her. Can't stand up . . . can't move . . . breathe. I have to save—

Lights are on me. Where are they coming from? Getting closer. Coming toward me. Can't move. Can't stop them. Didn't think I'd die like this, lying on the ground, not able to move . . .

The lights stop in front of me.

"Get him in the car!" someone yells. "Now!"

"He's coming!" yells someone else.

I'm lifted up and put in the backseat. Someone falls on me. "We're in! Go!" We're moving. The person stays on top of me. I try to tell them I'm having a hard enough time breathing without them sitting on me, but all that comes out is a squeaky whistle.

"Bright Boy!" someone is yelling. "Bright Boy!"

I try to answer, but I can't. The yelling seems so far away, like they're at the far end of a long tunnel, and I'm too tired to answer them. Too tired. Let me sleep . . . let me slee—

"SCOTT!"

My eyes open for a second. I try to see the face of the person sitting on me, but it's in shadow.

"SCOTT! I'm going to give you something! Don't fight it!"

I open my mouth to say I'm too tired to fight. OW! He jams something into my neck! I thrash.

"Stop him!" someone yells from the front seat.

"I can't!" yells the guy on top of me. "He's too strong!"

"Scott!" yells the driver. "We're saving you! Calm down!"

"Give him the sedative!" comes another voice.

"I did!"

I try to keep fighting . . . but I can't . . . I stop . . . I can't move . . . I can't . . .

"He's right behind us!" someone yells

"Get us out of here!!" yells the guy on top of me.

"Hold on!" yells the driver.

I feel the pull of acceleration, but I'm fading. I can't stay awake. I don't want to die like this . . .

19

I JOLT AWAKE . . . LIKE SOMEONE

flicked my switch from off to on. I'm in a bed in a tastefully decorated bedroom . . . all dark colors and dark wood furniture. Trace amounts of light are seeping into the room through the heavy curtains. My arms are secured to the sides of the bed. I can't raise them past my chest. I feel too weak to snap the restraints.

"Scott?"

I look across the room. Someone is sitting in a chair facing me, but because of the lack of light, I can't see who it is.

"Scott?"

"Who are you?" I croak. My throat feels like it's stuffed with Styrofoam.

"Would you like something to drink?" the person asks.

"You have five seconds to tell me who you are before I snap these restraints and break your neck."

He stands up, and takes a few steps toward me. I must still be unconscious, because the closer the person gets to me, the more he looks like Jake Berkshire.

"Jake?" I ask.

"Yes," he says.

"Am I dead?" I ask.

Jake smiles. "No. You're—"

I snap the restraint and grab his neck in one fluid motion. "Then where am I? And what the hell is going on? Five seconds. Four . . . three . . ."

"This is not a dream. You are not dead. It really is me, Jake Berkshire . . . your 'bully' from school, and I just saved your life. Will you please put me down so I can explain?" Jake spoke all this without moving his lips. It was like his voice was projected over a loudspeaker inside my head.

I put him down. I use my free hand to snap the other restraint. My legs are not restrained, so I swing them over the side of the bed. I try to stand up, but the world tilts at an uncomfortable angle. I sit back down on the bed.

"What did you do to me?" I ask.

"Side effects from the antidote."

"Antidote? To what?"

"There's a lot to explain," he says.

"Allison. I have to—"

"You've been out for four hours. The battle is long over. Sit back. Let me get you some water. You need to rest."

"No, I . . ."

"Scott," Jake says, his voice in my head again. "You need to trust me. I've been watching over you for a while now. We have a lot to do, and not a lot of time, but the only way to do it is to do it right. I know you're worried about Allison . . . but if you decide to bust out of here without a plan, you will die. And then you'll be no help to anyone. *Capisce?*"

"Yes. Now get out of my head."

"OK," he says, this time with his mouth. "You want some water?"

I nod. He hands me a bottle. I take a sip.

"You're a plus/plus, aren't you?" I ask.

"Just one plus. Intelligence. Minor telepathy. Minor telekinesis. But those'll get stronger as I get—"

"Wait. Stop. What—?" I have so many questions, I don't even know which to ask first.

"To answer the first question on your mind right now: No, I'm not really a bully, and I'm not an idiot, but I guess you've already figured that out. As for the why . . . well, to protect you, of course."

"Protect me? From what?"

He laughs. "From yourself. And some other people, as it turns out . . . but we'll get to that."

"You're not—" I start.

"Making any sense?" he finishes.

"Stop—"

"Finishing your sentences? Sorry about that. Can't help it, I'm afraid. Comes with the territory."

"Yeah, well, it's—"

"Annoying," Jake says. "I know. I try to cut back. Anyway, you're wondering why you would possibly need protection from yourself, right? Do you know how many times you almost gave up your secret identity? Hm?"

"Uhh . . . none?" I say.

He smiles. "Of course, you don't notice. I'm not blaming you, or trying to be condescending. It's just . . . well, you've got a lot going on. You don't always notice when some cute girl is going to ask you out, or when someone who has been looking at your picture in the paper or on the news all morning sees you in school and suddenly puts two and two together."

"That never—I wear a—"

"Mask. Right. Look, that whole mask thing may work in the comics, but it does absolutely zip in the real world," Jake says. He takes a sip from his water. "You wear a mask, yet everything else about you is the same. And with the advent of digital photography, and the crystal clear images they're been able to get of you lately, it's much easier to see the person behind the mask. You may still fool some people, but more and more are catching on. That's where I come in."

"But you're a jerk to me."

"And you've had to take it, otherwise you were afraid people would find out you were Bright Boy. You had no idea how right you were."

"What do you mean?"

"Oh my God . . . so many incidents, I can hardly remember . . . I mean, not really . . . I remember everything, but cataloguing all the moments that you didn't notice will do nothing to convince you. Either you believe me, or you don't."

"I don't know what I believe right now," I say.

"Fair enough. Take it from me, you almost let your

guard down at least four times a week. Sometimes more. Then me and my idiot crew swoop in and humiliate you—"

"So that I look like a wimp."

"Ahh . . . see? Finishing other people's sentences is fun, right?"

"But come on . . . if some kid was going to see my face and put the whole thing together, wouldn't they think that this was part of an act to throw them off the trail?"

Jake smiles. "Those are the ones I recruit." He points to the door. His "idiot" friends are standing there. They smile at me. Jimmy Douglas waves. "Are you OK?" Jimmy asks. "You scared the bejeebers out of us."

"The bejeebers? Are you kidding?" I ask.

"I don't like to cuss," Jimmy says.

"Every other word out of your mouth is usually a swear word!" I yell.

Shane and Andrew start laughing and teasing Jimmy, and Jimmy takes it all with a good-natured grin. The teasing is friendly, so unlike the way they tease me in school.

"All right, guys," Jake says. "Out. He and I need to talk."

They start to leave. Jimmy comes over to me and gives

me one of the most sincere hugs I've ever received. He looks at me with tears in his eyes. "We're so happy you're OK," he says, then leaves, sniffling.

"He's a huge softy," Jake says.

"He once gave me a wedgie and hung me on a hook by my underwear." I say.

"Yup. And then he locked himself in his room and bawled his eyes out for two days straight. He called in sick to school. We had to bust down the door to get to him . . . tell him that he did it to protect you. He came around, but vowed to never physically hurt you again."

"I . . . I can't—"

"It's OK. We knew this would be weird for you. But you have to hang in there. We haven't even gotten started yet." He pulls a laptop out of the backpack at his feet.

"Look, this is all really interesting, and thanks for all the saves . . . but I have to get out of here," I say, steadying myself to walk. "My whole world just—"

"—went nuclear," he says. "Yeah, I know. Quickly, tell me what happened."

"I was with . . . a girl . . ."

"Allison Mendes, aka Monkeywrench," he says.

When he says her name, I remember Allison holding my hand and looking scared, trying to catch her breath.

My stomach tightens up. I start to rock back and forth with restless energy. "I have to go." I stand up and head for the door.

"SCOTT!" he yells, with his mouth and his mind. "You NEED to stay focused. I know you don't want to hear this, but if she's still alive, you're not going to help her by rushing in and getting yourself killed! Then she's definitely dead! Do you understand?"

"Yes." Stay focused. Just like Louis taught you . . . but thinking about Louis is like ripping off another scab. I close my eyes and take a deep breath. Focus. "Yes," I say again, this time with a little more force. I turn and sit back down on the bed across from Jake.

"Good. Now tell me what happened."

I tell him everything . . . the whole story about Allison and me, my outfit, the phone call and Phantom turning on me, watching Allison trying to breathe . . . all of it. And I don't know if Jake is good or bad . . . if he really saved me, or if he's trying to set me up. And really, I don't care. All I know is that I have to tell someone. "Phantom tried to kill me," I say, "and I still have no idea why."

"Do you even know what you were hit with?"

"Some kind of dart, I don't know."

"It's adrenaline."

"Adrenaline? Seriously? Come on . . . there's no way that a shot of adrenaline would kill me."

He turns his laptop around. There's a picture of a man lying in an alley. "Does he look familiar?"

"Should he?"

"Well, you have fought him roughly a dozen times."

I look at the picture a little closer, but I can't seem—

"He's a personal trainer. His name is Justin Wheeler. You knew him as Rogue Warrior."

My mouth hangs open.

"His body was found in an alley downtown earlier today," Jake says. "He had massive a heart attack. His adrenaline levels had spiked through the roof."

"He was on steroids."

"His heart literally exploded in his chest. Steroids wouldn't do that."

"How do you know this?"

"My dad performed the autopsy."

"Your father?"

"Not important right now. Look here." He boxes off the section of the photo that has Warrior's neck in it and magnifies it so it fills the screen. "See that little pinprick right there?"

"Barely."

"Exactly. If we weren't specifically looking for it, we would have missed it. Sound familiar?"

I put my hand up to my neck. "How did you know to look for it?"

"Again, not important right now. Here's the thing," Jake says, "the reason you plus/plus, speed and strengths, are the way you are is because you were born with really dense, heavy bones. They're A LOT heavier than normal human bones. Your muscles had to adapt to be stronger, have more elasticity. The older you get, the bigger your bones get, and the stronger and faster you become."

"Wait . . . the report said that I get stronger, but not faster."

He smiles. "You read the report?"

I nod.

"Yeah, well, they got some stuff right," he says, "but not everything. And that's kind of the way we want it."

"Who's we?" Before Jake can answer, I say it for him. "I know . . . not important right now. So . . . I'm going to get stronger *and* faster than I am now?"

"Yup, but here's the problem: It seems that some of your organs are pretty much regular, old, run-of-the-mill organs. Your heart has somewhat adapted to the additional strain you put on it, but it hasn't completely adapted. It's still very similar to the heart of an average person, except the average person isn't jumping off buildings or trying to lift a car over their head."

A light goes on in my head. "So . . . a shot of adrenaline takes my heart, which is under strain as it is, and pushes it right over the edge."

"Correct. You just survived your first heart attack," he says. "Congratulations."

"Thanks a ton."

"There was something weird about that dart, though."

"What?"

"The adrenaline inside was a slow-release formula. Enough up front to take you out of action and give you some of the effects of full-blown cardiac arrest, but not enough to push you over the edge. Now, if you didn't get the antidote, you'd have died within half an hour."

I shudder.

"But it seems like whoever designed the dart gave you some time to get away," he says. "Here, take a look at this picture of Warrior again. See how his eyes are distended. His heart looked like a burst water balloon. Whoever hit you didn't give Rogue Warrior the same deal."

"Who—?

"Well, it's either Phantom Justice or Dr. Chaotic," Jake says. "They've been working together for years."

It takes a moment for it to sink in. "Wait—what?! No, they haven't."

"All right . . . really quickly, because we need time to figure out our next move," he says. "Phantom isn't really a superhero like you think he is. He's in it for the money. Large companies hire him to fight battles over their products. He then hires the villains and stages everything. All those battles you've fought over the years? Yeah, those have all been elaborate ads."

"Wha—no! I wasn't—"

"Don't worry . . . if I thought you were in on it, we wouldn't be having this conversation. He used you. And now that you and Allison have been stealing the spotlight, it looks like Phantom and Chaotic decided to get rid of you . . . In fact"—Jake pauses as if a thought just hit him—"I bet they were annoyed about you and Allison at first, but then they saw a way to use it to their advantage."

"What do you mean?"

"Nothing pulls in the youth demographic like tragic romance."

"That's—I don't—that's not—"

Jake turns his laptop around again and flips quickly through a whole file full of pictures. It's like a "greatest hits" collection of Phantom's and my battles. And it doesn't take a genius to see what they all have in common . . . all the big battles took place near giant signs for products. Champion Motor Company, Can-do Cola, IGO Computers, and a ton of others.

"Yeah, but what—"

"About all the battles you had that didn't involve products?" Jake says. "Those fall into one of two categories: Either someone was auditioning for Phantom Justice, to see if they could win a slot on the roster of villains, or the villain you faced truly believed that the whole 'villain/superhero' thing was real, and Phantom had to defeat him in order to maintain his reputation. For the last group, Phantom usually recruited the ones who showed promise, and killed off the ones who didn't, so he wouldn't have to deal with them again."

I start shaking my head. I can't believe this. It was all hitting me too hard and too fast. "No . . . no . . ."

"I have one last thing to show you," Jake says. He clicks a button on his computer and a new picture pops up on his screen. It's a picture of Trent's house. "The explosion that Trent told you about . . . the one from

Dr. Chaotic's attack . . . it was a lie. These pictures were taken an hour ago." He flips through a bunch of pictures of the house. It looks the way it always has.

"He set you up," Jake says.

I don't want to believe it, but there's no other way to make the events of the past twelve hours add up. And the more I doubt it, the more I resist, the more time I'm wasting.

"So, do you think—"

"That Louis is still alive?" Jake says. "I don't know."

"Do you think . . ." I pause, expecting him to finish my sentence. Instead, he pauses.

"I don't know that, either. She's fallen off the grid, so to speak."

"I have to—"

"I know you do," Jake says. "You're lucky, though. Finding Allison is part of my plan."

20

"WHERE AM I GOING?" I ASK.

"I don't know yet," Jake says in my head.

"So should I stop?"

"No. Keep heading south."

I'm running across the rooftops of Manhattan, looking for the hidden lab of Dr. Chaotic. I'm restless and keyed up and on the verge of panic. I have this feeling that Allison's still alive, but that she won't be for long . . . and that I'm the only one who can save her . . . if I can only find the stupid lab.

"Don't freak out on me, Scott," Jake says.

"I'm not freaking out!" I yell.

"Right. Obviously."

"Where is it?" I ask.

"I don't know yet. Dr. Chaotic is the most powerful plus intelligence on the planet. Usually, I can pick something up from him, just floating around in the ether . . . but right now, I got nothing. He's throwing up some interference, I think."

"Great! So now what?"

"Where are you?"

"Lincoln Center."

"Keep moving south," he says.

"Why south?"

"Just a hunch."

In about seven minutes, I'm on the roof of the Flatiron Building.

"Scott? Where are you?"

"The Flatiron Building," I say. "Being a psychic, shouldn't you already know that?"

I hear him sigh. "I'm focusing on other things right now, like Dr. Chaotic and—uh-oh . . ."

"What?"

"Something is headed right for you!"

"What?!" I yell. "Where? I don't see anything?"

"I don't know yet . . . it's something big . . . filled with hate . . . rage . . . "

"Phantom Justice! But I don't see him!"

"He sees you."

"How do you know?"

"I just know!" he yells. "He's almost on you!"

I look around frantically. I don't see anything. I stop . . . focus . . . concentrate . . . close my eyes. A sound . . . like a sonic boom . . . from the left . . . behind me . . . I roll right, just as Phantom's fist flies through the spot where my head was.

"GRRRRAAAA!" he yells as he smashes right through one of the air-conditioning units on the roof. He's up in half a second.

"Scott! He's there!" Jake yells in my head.

"Yeah! Thanks!"

Phantom comes at me with a flurry of punches of kicks, some of which are coming so fast, I don't even see them. I don't know how, but I manage to avoid all of them.

"Scott!" Jake yells. "What's happening? Are you OK?"

"Jake! Stop! Talking!"

"Sorry!"

Phantom Justice stops trying to hit me. Now he's just swaggering toward me. I back up, trying to keep a distance between us. "Scott, you miserable little twerp. Look at you! You're not dead!" he says, almost cheerfully.

His eyes look mischievous and murderous at the same time. "You've got a little more stamina than I thought!"

He does a quick roundhouse kick. It isn't one of his more powerful ones, but it is fast . . . so fast that it manages to tag me in the jaw. He tries to follow it up with another kick, but I block it.

"What is wrong with you?!" I yell. "You're Phantom Justice! You're supposed to be a good guy!"

"I am a good guy," he says. "Just because I want to fire you doesn't make me a bad guy."

"You're trying to kill me!"

"Hey . . . you're not a cashier at the grocery store, you know. This is how you get fired from this job. And I would appreciate it if you took it like a man."

He comes at me in two quick strides, leading with a right cross. He's fast, but I manage to get my guard up. I realize too late that it was a feint. His left foot kicks me in the stomach. I fall over the back of one of the AC units. My head smacks against the ground. I feel like I'm going to puke. I shake my head to clear the cobwebs. He's coming to get me.

"Don't play possum with me," he says. "Come on!"

There's a broken broom handle on the ground right

beside me. I grasp it. He reaches down to grab me, and I slam the piece of wood into the side of his head. The handle shatters. His head snaps to the left and he drops me, but he doesn't fall. I somersault backward and get into my defense position. He slowly turns his head back toward me. He's smiling.

"Was that supposed to hurt?"

"What is your problem?" I yell at him.

"You keep asking me that, and I thought I already made it clear. My problem is you . . . has been for a while," he says. "I mean, after all I've done for you? I took you in. I fed you, clothed you, sent you to the finest school in the city. And this is how you repay me? Hm? By ruining a character that I created?"

"I'm not 'a character you created.'"

"You're right. You aren't. Bright Boy is. Bright Boy doesn't exist because of you; you exist because of Bright Boy. Got it?"

"Your whole life is a lie!"

He shrugs. "Yeah? So? So's yours, you just don't know it yet. But I wouldn't worry too much about it . . . you don't have a lot of time left." He throws a flurry of left and right jabs. I block and avoid, block and avoid, but he's going too fast. He's too strong. Three catch me in the face. *Bam, bam, bam.* Just like that, and my nose is bleeding.

"Do you want to be a hero?" He snaps out a right. I avoid it, but his left is too fast. It catches me in the ear, sending a bright spike of pain through my whole head. "Or would you rather die a sissy? Your choice."

I'm holding the side of my head. I try to block his punches, but I'm shaken . . . woozy . . . my head hurts. His left jab hits my cheek. I hit the ground, but immediately spring up again and catch him with a roundhouse kick, square in the face. He staggers back. He wasn't expecting that.

"Well, looks like you've got a little fight in you yet!" he says. "You're impressing me, Scott . . . and you haven't asked me any stupid 'Why are you doing it?' questions."

"It's obvious why you're doing it," I say. "You're just another lowlife scumball looking for money."

"Ha! It's adorable that you think I shouldn't be proud of that. Our battles move product, and companies pay money for that. Lots of it. How else is a superhero supposed to make some scratch? Do you think the public wants to pay for all the good deeds we do? Huh? No! They want us to save them, but they want us to do it for free."

"Yeah! Because we're heroes!"

He laughs and shakes his head. "Scott, heroes still need to buy houses. We still need food. That stuff ain't free, kid. Come on, man, don't make me lose respect for you."

"Hey, psychopath," I say, "I couldn't care less if you respect me or not. You know, most kids at school laugh at you. That whole 'I am the darkness' thing is just a big joke. And that whisper-growl you think is so mysterious. HA! Sooo lame . . ."

"Oh yeah . . . like I'm going to care what a bunch of brainless little schoolkids think."

"You care. Look at you. You're twitching. You know what they call you? Do you? They call you Phantom Jerkface?"

"Whoa, Scott. You're on fire!" Trent says. "You figured out that I'm an egocentric sociopath, so you preyed on my vanity! And it stung! Ooo! Very impressive! Buuuut, I guess now it's my turn." He pauses, a malicious smile creeping across his face. "I watched your little girlfriend die. She suffered. A lot."

My jaw clenches, but I don't yell. My fist quivers, but I don't punch him. He's probably lying. He's trying to get under my skin, get me to make a mistake, but I'm not going to let him. I think of Louis, and focus on what he taught me.

"Don't worry, though," Trent says. "I made sure I gave her a little kiss good-b—"

CRACK.

My right fist hits him. I honestly don't remember throwing it. It must've been pretty fast, because he didn't see it coming . . . for that matter, neither did I. The only reason I know I hit him is because my knuckles are tingling and his lip is bleeding.

He looks worried. How did I hit him? He's supposed to be faster than me. "Ooo . . . Bright Boy is angry! You're snarling!" he says, his look of doubt gone. "Who knows? Maybe if you were this fired up earlier, you might've been able to save her . . . but, oh well."

I feel something snap in my head. I can even hear the sound it makes: a loud *crack,* like a baseball bat breaking in half. "Say something else," I say. "Please."

"Ha! Why? Because you think your righteousness is going to give you power? Hm? Fine. You know what her dying words wer—"

CRACK. His head snaps back again, and a little blood dribbles out from the corner of his mouth.

"No," I say. "And neither do you."

The look of doubt is back. He wipes his mouth with the back of his hand. "Sure I do," he says, trying to recover the advantage. "I was there. She said, 'Scott is a gullible little—'"

WHAM!

OK, that one wasn't me. A blast from above us nails Trent and sends him flying backward. My heart skips a little. I turn to look. Sure enough, it's Dr. Chaotic in his propulsion boots and he has some sort of complex-looking weapon pointed at Trent. He's alone.

"You idiot!" Trent yells at Chaotic. "I knew it! I knew you'd throw it all away for that stupid little girl!"

Chaotic fires his weapon again, but this time Trent is able to avoid it. He leaps and lands a flying hammer punch to Chaotic's face, sending him flying off at a weird angle. Chaotic lands on the roof with a sickening thud. Trent races over to finish him off, but Chaotic is up again and waiting for him. Chaotic grabs him and flings him off the roof. Chaotic then zips over to me.

"Is Jake there?" he asks.

"Yes," Jake says in my head. I'm guessing that Chaotic can hear it in his head, too, because he nods. "Got it! Scott, we have to go."

"No, wait!" I yell.

"No time!" Jake yells back. "Go! Get off the roof."

"No! Enough with this psychic garbage!" I grab Dr. Chaotic. I shake him. He doesn't resist. "Is she still alive? TELL ME SHE'S STILL ALIVE!"

His eyes look puffy. His face looks tired and empty, as if he's spent the last of his energy and is now just running on fumes. "Bear always told you the truth," he says.

"Wait . . . What? What are you—"

"And he always will."

Jake starts yelling. "SCOTT!"

"What are you talking about?!" I yell at Chaotic. "Is Louis still alive? Is Allison? Tell me!"

"SCOTT! GET OUT OF THERE RIGHT—"

Too late. Trent rams Dr. Chaotic and me, knocking us over like paper dolls. Trent is moving so fast, he skids on the roof, stops himself, and turns and charges again. Chaotic springs up and faces him like a bullfighter. He pulls out a gun . . . the same dart gun they used on me . . . and Allison. Trent stops.

"Scott?" Jake asks.

"Yeah."

"Oh good . . . you're still alive . . . NOW GET IT IN GEAR!"

"Not yet."

Trent is staring at Dr. Chaotic and me with a sick grin on his face. He chuckles, but it's grim; there's no humor in it. "Would you look at this: my greatest enemy and my old sidekick, together. Pretty ironic . . . and convenient. Well, for me a least. See, after I kill you both, all I have to do is say you offed each other. Might have to move your bodies around, but it's not like I haven't done *that* before."

Chaotic lifts his dart gun. "You're not killing anyone else."

Phantom laughs. "HA! Who's going to stop me? You? You've got the smarts, Edward, but you're lacking in everything else. Maybe . . . just maybe . . . a triple-plus could've stopped me . . . your daughter perhaps . . . but, well, we all know how that turned out."

I look over at Chaotic. He's not saying anything. His face has gotten tight. Tears start to form in his eyes.

I turn to Trent. "Allison was—?"

"A triple plus?" Trent says. "That's right, Bright Boy! In fact, there are only two triple pluses in the whole world—right, Edward?"

I look back at Chaotic. Tears are streaming down his face.

"But Allison's strictly past tense, isn't she?" Trent says. "So, I guess that leaves just me."

What?! I look over. Chaotic's eyes are as wide as mine.

"You?" Chaotic says.

Trent does a little bow. "Strongest, fastest, smartest. So smart that I trumped *you* . . . I'm telling you now because, well, I want the last thought in your head to be that I outsmarted you, the great Dr. Chaotic. Of course, the second-to-last thought in your head is that I killed your daughter. Not a great week for the ol' doctor, huh?" He chuckles.

Chaotic presses a button on his forearm. There's an electrical hum as something under his outfit powers up. He starts to glow.

Trent laughs. "Oh, this should be fun. Hope you charged your batteries, Edward. Oh, and say hello to your sweet daughter for me when you see her again . . . in about four minutes."

I've had enough. Triple plus or not, I'm going to knock Trent's face off his skull. I cock my fists and start toward him, but before I get more that one step, Dr. Chaotic grabs me. "He's mine," he says, then flings me off the roof.

All I manage to get out is a quick "Hey—" before I'm airborne.

Jake is immediately in my head. "Scott. Listen to me. Chaotic threw you off the roof because you're the only hope of beating Phantom. You have to head south, right now."

"Can I not die first?" I ask.

"Sure. But hurry up."

I grab FP-75, swing myself around, and fling myself onto the nearest rooftop. I can hear the sounds of Trent and Chaotic battling behind me. "You and Chaotic had a 'meeting of the minds,' right?" I ask.

"I know what you're going to ask."

"Good. Then answer."

"Allison is not our concern right now. Our concern is keeping you alive and stopping Phantom Justice."

"Well, maybe I should go back and ask Chaotic myself," I say.

"Stop being such an idiot, OK? He won't be able to hold Phantom off for long."

"But he has that armor, and a dart gun. Maybe he'll—"

"He won't. Phantom's too fast," Jake says. "Chaotic'll never be able to hit him, even with the enhanced speed of the armor. No, you're it."

"That whole thing about Louis . . . what do you think he meant?"

"I don't know. All I do know is that you have to go where I tell you."

"Fine. Where?"

"Brooklyn . . . to Dr. Chaotic's lab."

21

IT TAKES ME EIGHT MINUTES TO
make it from the Flatiron District across the Manhattan
Bridge to Brooklyn. I'm standing on the roof of the
DUMBO Arts Center. I turn and look at the Brooklyn
Bridge, and Manhattan beyond it. This is Allison's
favorite view from the other side. Seeing it now makes
me feel empty.

I can picture Allison's face as she looked at it, as if
this was the only place on the planet where she could
find peace. I remember thinking that I wanted to help
her look like that all the time.

I need to find her.

But what if I find her, and she's . . .

I'm wondering if I really want to know. If she's gone, will I be able to handle it?

"I don't know," Jake says in my head, "but that's a question for later. Right now, Phantom has to be stopped and the only way to do that is for you to get to the lab."

"Seriously . . . you being the voice of my conscience is really surreal."

"One mile south on Jay Street is the New York City College of Technology. Get there. And hurry up, jerkface. He's coming," Jake barks in his best bully voice. "Is that better?"

"Oddly enough, yes. Right now, I'll take anything that feels normal, even if it's you being mean to me."

I turn and start sprinting across rooftops. The moment where my life changes is less than five minutes away. I keep sprinting anyway.

"OK," I say. "I'm here. At the college. Now what?"

"Find the library building. Go inside."

"Uh, hello . . . it's two in the morning. It's closed."

Jake sighs. "You just got here, from Manhattan, by leaping from rooftop to rooftop. Also, the majority of your thoughts, at this very moment, are directed toward figuring out how to kill Trent when you see him again.

So what exactly is holding you back from breaking into a library: your ability or your morals?"

I head for the ground, spy a building with columns and a telltale library sign on the front, get a running start, then go crashing through the front door. There's no alarm. "Huh. OK . . . now what? Is there a secret bookshelf or a trapdoor or something?"

"Get in the elevator and press the basement button."

"Seriously?"

"Do it!"

I do as I'm told. The elevator goes down one floor to the basement.

"Now wait for the doors to open again," Jake says, "then close."

"OK."

"Now quickly, hit the buttons in this order: five-two-four-three-five-four-five-four-three-two-one-three-four-three-four-three-four-five-six-four-three-two-one-one-three-four—"

Jake is rattling off numbers as fast as he can speak them. I stop trying to think about it, because if I think, I'll make a mistake. I just react, pressing the numbers as fast he says them.

"Five-four-one," Jake says, then stops.

"Is that it?"

"Why? What happened?"

"Nothing," I say.

"Maybe we got one wrong."

"OK," I say, sighing, "Let's try it again."

"Five—"

The elevator plummets down at a force and speed that start to lift me off the ground.

"Scott?"

"Wait!" I say, and just manage to stop the vomit rising in my throat. "Is this the only way to get down here?"

"No, but it's the quickest."

The elevator comes to a dead stop. I slam against the floor but immediately spring back up. The doors start to open. I'm queasy, from both my nerves and that elevator ride, but I rush out anyway.

"Allison!" I shout as I run from room to room. The place is big, but split up into a lot of smaller rooms. Some of the rooms are crammed with so much junk that I can't even open the door. Others are completely empty. "ALLISON!"

"It's an old testing lab," Jake says without me

having to ask the obvious question. "They put it a mile underground, so that if anything went wrong . . ." He trails off without finishing the sentence.

"What were they testing?"

"You don't want to know."

"You're right. ALLISON!"

I crash through a door, and find myself in a much larger room than the rest. It's as big as an airplane hangar. The junk in here is newer, and I recognize some of it. These are Dr. Chaotic's old weapons. His desk is set off by a bunch of work lamps. There's a plate with a moldy sandwich on it, but the mold is fairly recent. There's a bunch of bookcases, with books, tools, and junk stuffed haphazardly into them. One shelf has a bunch of remote control cars and stuffed animals on it, in various states of deconstruction. A teddy bear smiles lazily at me from the shelf.

I start running through the room, looking for something, anything to indicate that Allison was here recently. "ALLISON!" When I don't find anything, I start throwing stuff around, looking for clues . . . a secret passage . . . anything . . . "ALLISON!"

"Scott," Jake says. "Scott! Listen to me!"

I ignore him.

"SCOTT!! You have to listen to me."

I don't.

"LISTEN TO ME! LISTEN TO ME! LISTEN TO ME! LISTEN TO ME! LISTEN TO ME!" starts blaring on endless loop in my head.

"Ow! All right! I'm here!"

"Scott . . . you need to stop. You'll find her later."

"No, I'll find her"—I stop—"now."

I found her.

"Scott . . ." Jake says.

I walk toward her, slowly.

"Scott . . . I'm so sorry."

She's lying in a glass-lidded coffin. The glass is cool to the touch, and the clinical part of my brain knows that it's because her father is keeping her cold . . . to preserve her. The hopeful idiot part of my brain suggests that she could be just resting . . . recovering from her injuries in some sort of stasis. But I've seen enough bodies in my time to know when one still has life in it, and when one doesn't. That doesn't stop me from staring at her, wishing for a blink or a twitch or something, damn it! And I'm slapping my palms on the glass and I'm screaming and I want to rip her out of there and hold her and perform

CPR on her in a last-ditch attempt to revive her, but I know it won't . . . I know it can't . . . She's already . . . I'm lost.

I rest my forehead on the glass. It's cool, and the morbid side of me wonders if the glass on her side is just as cool as this.

"Scott!" Jake yells inside my head. "Come on, man, pull it together!"

"Yeah, come on, Bright Boy, pull it together."

I whip around. Phantom Justice is standing there, smiling at me.

"He's there!" Jake yells in my head. "He's there! How the he—?"

"Tell your accomplice to shut his yap," Phantom says in his whisper-growl. "He's giving me a headache."

"Accomplice?" I ask. "What are you talking about?"

"You've thwarted justice long enough, Bright Boy . . . and to think, I trusted you!"

"What?! What are you—?!" I yell . . . and then it clicks. I look around, and there they are—cameras. Four of them, tracking our every movement.

"How could you kill Louis," Phantom says, "after all he did for you?"

"So that's how it's going to go down?" I ask.

Phantom gives me a look and a half-smile that tells me that's exactly how it's going to go down.

I think about Chaotic's last words to me . . . about Bear always telling me the truth. "He always will," he had said. I think about Allison, and how I accused her of lying to me, right before she—

I pick up a heavy piece of metal from Chaotic's desk.

"You're going to need more than that to defeat the power of justi—"

Before Trent can finish, I throw the piece of metal at one of the cameras. All that's left of it is a sparking wire and a pile of glass and plastic on the ground.

"Scott!" Jake yells in my head. "What are you doing?! You're killing my feed!"

"I'm sick of it," I say. I fling another piece of metal at another one of the cameras, destroying it. "Sick of the games . . . the lying . . ."

Another piece of metal . . . *SMASH!* Another camera falls to the ground in a hail of broken plastic. Three down.

"This, right here, is going to be about the truth," I say. "I want to see your real face, Phantom 'Justice.' You at least owe me that much."

I smash the last camera.

Phantom smiles. "Whatever you say, Bright Boy," he hisses.

"Uh, you do know that those cameras were the only things keeping him from killing you!" Jake yells at me.

"I doubt it," I say. "Right, Trent?"

"Smart kid," he answers, but there's not a trace of Phantom Justice in his voice now. It's just me and Trent. "Ready to join your little girlfriend?"

I'm looking around the room for a weapon . . . *any* weapon . . .

"Like the spare dart gun?" Trent asks. He points at the desk to my right. "Third drawer up on the left. I find it particularly torturous when a person knows that their saving grace is right there, within arm's reach, and they still can't get to it. Just makes the moment more . . . delicious. You know what I mean?"

I look at the desk. If I go for the drawer, he'll slam it shut and probably chop my hand off.

"Probably wouldn't work even if you had it," he says, laughing. "I'm too fast. Just ask Dr. Chaotic. Oh wait . . . you can't."

My mind is racing, trying to formulate a plan . . . any kind of plan.

"Here's the thing, Scott. I'm going to kill you. There's

nothing you can do about it. Now, if you give me a good enough challenge—if you *earn* your death—I'll put you in a nice little pose with your girlfriend, so all the little teenyboppers can scream their little heads off about how *romantic* this whole thing was. But if you suck . . . if you're an embarrassment to the training I gave you . . . well, let's just say, there won't be much of you left."

"Are you going to bore me to death? Is that your plan?" I growl, and take a couple of steps toward him.

He smiles, nods slightly, then comes at me with a vicious right hand. I push him to my right so his momentum carries him past me. I slip behind him. His left is fast enough to clip me in the ribs. Trent follows up with a right toward my head. I leap over it, because I know if I duck, he'd come at me with a kick, and I'd be too off balance to block it.

I land, ready to defend, but he's stopped attacking. Instead, he stands there, bouncing in his fighter's stance, smiling that creepy, sociopathic smile of his. "Not bad," he says. "Are you going to attack, though, or are you going to be a total sissy about—"

I cut him off with a left to his face. It glances off him, but the look of surprise he gives me is worth it.

"Looks like we're picking up where we left off

earlier," I say. "You remember earlier, when I hit you so fast you couldn't defend yourself?"

He laughs, but he can't hide the look of concern on his face. "If those are the 'cotton balls' you're going to hit me with, then feel free to be the fastest. A few thousand of them *might* slow me down."

I try a left roundhouse kick, but he sidesteps and kicks out my support leg. Before I can move, he lifts me off my feet.

"Well, that was a disappointment," he says, holding me up by the front of my shirt.

I walk up the front of him until my foot is standing on his face. I bite his hand and push off his face with my foot, backflipping out of his grip.

"AGHHH!" he yells. "Biting? I did NOT teach you to bite! I think that deserves a little punishment."

He runs at me. I steel myself for impact, but he leaps and flips over me. By the time I figure out what he's up to, it's too late . . . he's already standing in front of Allison's coffin.

"Killing you just doesn't seem like punishment enough," he says. He smashes his fist against the glass. It starts to crack.

"Stop!" I yell.

"No," he says, and smashes the glass again. The crack gets larger.

"STOP!"

I start toward him. He hits the glass again. This time it shatters. He pulls Allison's body out. His face is crazed. He's smiling at me. He strolls to the center of the room. I'm frozen.

"Well, here we are at the end," he says. "There are so many ways to do this, I just can't decide. I wonder what your 'fans' will say when they find your body and cradled lovingly in your lifeless arms is Allison's decapitated head." He starts laughing.

My teeth are clenched. My fists are closed into tight balls and shaking. Red light is creeping in along the edges of my vision, closing into a tunnel, with Trent in the center. Everything else in the world falls away except for Trent, and my hatred for him.

He sneers at me. "I'm going to tear your girlfriend to pieces, Bright Boy, and there's not a thing you can do about—"

I rush him, slamming into his midsection. We go tumbling, our limbs tangled. Allison's body goes flying. I'm all rage and fury, elbows and knees. My right elbow smashes his eye. "Gahh!" he says, and that just makes me go faster. He's trying to push me off him, but I'm moving too fast for him to get a grip. My left knee hits his nose.

"AAAAA!" he screams in pain and frustration, and I just keep whirling, twisting, punching, kicking, thrashing. He's screaming. He gets lucky and manages to grab my arm. He flings me away. I roll and pop up, and I'm back into my stance. Trent is standing where I left him. His nose is bleeding. His left eye is swollen shut. It's not enough. I want to pound on his face. I want the coroner to need dental records.

"You . . . little . . . PUNK!" he screams, blood and spittle flying out of his mouth. "You don't TOUCH me!"

I stand and stare at him. A sound bubbles out of the back of my throat. It sounds like a growl. But I don't rush him. That won't work twice.

Trent wipes his nose with the back of his hand, then takes a deep breath . . . shakes his head . . . composes himself . . . gets back into control. He pulls what looks like a remote control out of his belt and points it at me. "Edward's design was a little clunky. Mine is small but lethal. Same dart as before, but you've already had the antidote, and unfortunately for you, it doesn't work twice. You fought well, but in the end, it never mattered. I was always going to win."

My muscles tense. I have to time this perfectly. Commit and move too early, and he'll track me. Move too late, and well, duh . . . His thumb is poised over the trigger button. My eyes are locked on the gun. He presses his thumb down, but not all the way. I flinch. He laughs. He presses with his thumb again. I flinch again. "Good-bye, Scott. You won't be missed."

His thumb starts pressing the button all the way down. I get ready to leap.

"HA-HA-HA-HA-HA!" The laugh comes out of nowhere and echoes through the room. Trent freezes. It wasn't my laugh, or his . . . it was Monkeywrench's. "Hey! Phantom Jerkface!"

Trent looks away from me for a second. I use it. I roll away, pick up a piece of metal on the floor, and fling it. It hits the remote in his hand, knocking it toward him. It fires into Trent's chin.

"Gahhh!" he says, falling to his knees. The convulsions start before the dart even dissolves.

"Ooooo! Klutzy!" Monkeywrench calls out, then starts laughing again.

I forget about Trent and start looking around the room for her. Because of the echoes, I can't track where her voice is coming from. "Allison!" I shout. "Where are you?"

She lands right next to Trent. She's wearing her older costume, the one where the mask covers more of her face . . . the one where I can't tell that if it's Allison or not.

"Allison?" I say.

Monkeywrench just stands there, without answering. She looks at Trent, then looks back at me.

Trent is wheezing, clawing at his chest, trying to crawl away. Monkeywrench puts her foot on his back and pushes him flat. She laughs again. He takes something out of his belt. It's a glass vial. I'm guessing it's the antidote. Monkeywrench guesses that, too . . . so she steps on it. The glass crunches beneath her foot. "Whoops-a-daisy," she says. "Oh, and you want to know what's realllly delicious? The fact that you got outsmarted by Bright Boy! And he's not even a plus intelligence! HA-HA-HA-HA!" She kneels down and grabs Trent's face, squeezing his cheeks. She turns his head toward the bookcase, and the smiley bear sitting innocently on one of the shelves. "Smile at the hidden camera! I'm guessing that the Internet is going to find the whole ripping-a-dead-girl's-head-off particularly interesting, don't you? HA-HA-HA-HA!"

She drops his face as if she can't stand touching it anymore.

I take a tentative step toward her. She stands up and faces me. My heart is thudding in my chest. "Allison?"

Her smile falters. Her eyes get moist and glassy. I take another step toward her.

Trent twists under her foot. Something rolls out of his hand. It's a flash grenade. Monkeywrench leaps toward me, pushing me out of the way a split second before the grenade explodes. I try to grab her, but she slips through my arms. There's an enormous *BOOM,* and the world goes white.

Smoke is everywhere. Lab equipment lies broken all around me. "Allison!" I shout. "ALLISON!" I can't see anything. I crawl to my feet. "Allison!"

"SCOTT!" Jake's voice is in my head. "SCOTT!"

"Jake? Where are you?"

"Behind you."

There's a swarm of people in HazMat suits behind

him; they start going through the wreckage. Maybe later I'll ask who they are, but right now, I don't care.

I go back to yelling. "Allison!"

"Scott! You need to stop this . . . come on, man."

"She was here!" I shout, and keep looking.

"I know."

"No! Not her body! She was here! Alive! Dressed as Monkeywrench! She distracted Trent so I could take him out. Then she saved me when Trent tried to blow us up. She knocked me clear."

"Are you sure it was Allison?" he asks.

"Well . . . no . . . her face was completely covered. But . . . she moved like Allison."

"Scott—"

"I have to find her."

"Not like this. Come on, man . . . let the professionals do it. If she's under all this, they'll find her."

"Fine. But I'm not leaving here until this whole place is—"

"Sir," one of the HazMat suits calls from across the room. "We found something."

2 2

I'M KNEELING ON THE FLOOR BESIDE

her. She looks exactly the same as she did in the coffin, except now there's some dirt in her hair. I'm trying to brush it out with my fingers, but it's not coming out. I keep brushing.

Jake comes walking over. "The camera was in the stuffed bear, just like you said. Was that what Chaotic meant when he talked about Bear telling the truth?"

I nod.

"Heck of a catch, Scott. Really," he says. "I've already sent the video out to every news source around the globe. We don't know what happened to Phantom yet, but even if he did get away, he's done."

I nod, but I don't really care. Not right now. Maybe later. I keep brushing.

Jake puts his hand on my shoulder. "You need to get out of here, Scott. Just go take a walk or something."

"I can't leave her."

"She's gone, man . . . there's nothing—"

"I can't leave her!" I keep brushing.

A woman in a HazMat suit comes over. "There's no one else here, sir."

Jake sighs, then wipes his hand over his face. "Let's wrap it up, then."

"Yes, sir," the woman says. "What do you want us to do about—?" She motions her head toward Allison.

I look up at the woman. She avoids looking back at me.

"Nothing," Jake says.

"Yes, sir," she responds, then turns and walks toward the other suits.

Jake squeezes my shoulder. "We'll be upstairs. Exit Four. When you're ready."

I nod without looking at him.

His hand leaves my shoulder. I can hear the footsteps behind me as everyone leaves.

I cradle Allison's head in my arms and start to cry.

I snap awake. My nose is all stuffed up. My eyes feel swollen. I don't know if I've fallen asleep or blacked out. I don't know if I've been here a couple of minutes or a couple of days. The lighting in this place is the same as it was before, but it's a mile underground, so that doesn't tell me anything. All I know is that I have to get out of here right now.

I pick Allison up and head for Exit Four. After about a half-mile of sprinting through a tunnel, then climbing up ten flights of stairs, I come to a couple of doors. I kick them open and step through; I'm standing in the middle of an old warehouse. It looks a lot like the one where Allison and I first found each other . . . really found each other.

Jake is there, but he's alone. He looks at me, but doesn't say a word.

I lay Allison on the ground at his feet.

Suddenly, I can't breathe. I feel suffocated. I can't be in here.

Jake is nodding. I see the word *GO* in giant letters in my mind.

I sprint for the doors to the outside . . . crash through

them without slowing down. I'm outside. It's sunny, which feels like a personal insult. I look around.

There it is. The Brooklyn Bridge.

I leap onto one of the lower rooftops and sprint and leap my way to the river. When I get to it, part of me wants to keep going . . . jump into the river and swim back to Manhattan. I skid to a stop a foot before the water and fall to my knees. I scream, but I'm too weak to put anything behind it.

I'd cry, but I feel dried out.

I look out at the bridge. I can feel it mocking me, for believing this could've ended any other way.

23

"YOU'RE GOING TO NEED TO GO BACK to school eventually," Jake says. "It's been three weeks."

I'm lying on a bed in the room over the Berkshires' garage. I've been here since . . .

"And you're going to have to eat a little more than one peanut butter and jelly sandwich every two days, especially if you expect to head into the city and run around."

He looks at me as if he expects me to be embarrassed that I've spent every night of the past three weeks scouring the city for Monkeywrench. I look at him and think about just what he can do with his expectations.

"Oh. OK," he says. "Thanks for the disturbing image."

I turn my attention back to the ceiling.

"What if you run into Phantom?" he asks.

I smile. "I'll ask him how the whole hero thing has been working out for him lately."

Things have not gone well for Trent over the past few weeks. The "stuffed bear video" has made it around the world several times over. All the major news networks, and most of the minor ones, have aired it. And it turns out that Monkeywrench was right: Most people had a pretty strong reaction to Trent's desire to rip the head off a dead girl. So first, Trent lost his "adoring public," and then he lost everything else. The Feds seized all of his assets, and now they're on standby, waiting for him to make a move. No one knows where he is.

"I still think going out there is a bad idea," Jake says.

"Tell me how you're involved in all this and I'll think about staying."

"No, you won't. You'll leave after I tell you."

"Maybe."

Jake sighs. I've been asking him this question every day for the past three weeks.

"My dad was a doctor for supers for years."

"Really?"

"Yeah."

"Huh. Well, that doesn't really explain why you have a bunch of people in HazMat suits at your beck and call," I say.

"The feds contacted my dad a few years ago. Bodies of plus/pluses started turning up . . . one by one."

"Why him? Why not call the supers?"

"The deaths all appeared medical in nature . . . accidental, or by natural causes, but they were starting to add up. The Feds wanted to keep it hush-hush until they could figure out what was going on. They didn't want a panic on their hands."

"That doesn't make sense," I say. "Unless they suspected that the deaths were actually murders, and they thought a super was committing them."

Jake smiles. "Kind of. They were suspicious, but it wasn't that cut and dry." He pauses. "Apart from the report on supers that you read, how much do you really know about your powers?" he asks.

I shrug. "I'm guessing by your question that I don't know as much as I think I know."

"Well, you already know about the heart thing . . . but there's something else: In physical plus/pluses like you, bone density starts to decrease at a certain age," he says. "The average is about 35 years old. You'll still have your powers, but your body won't be able to support them.

"It's like putting a Ferrari engine in a moped," he continues. "Fast and strong on the inside, really fragile on the outside. It's way too easy to have an accident, and most of those accidents are fatal."

"Oh. Well, that's depressing."

"So, most of the deaths my dad and I were investigating fell into two categories: heart attacks in young kids who accidentally pushed themselves too fast, too soon, and people thirty-five and older who met with some kind of unfortunate 'accident.'

"And some of them probably were accidental," he continues, "but about a month ago, my dad and I went through the old records. Guess what we found . . ."

"Unexplained needle marks on the heart attack kids," I say.

"Eighty-nine percent of them. And now we're thinking, who knows how many of those older pluses got 'accidentally' bumped in front of trains, or down a flight of stairs."

"But what happened to all the ones about in their prime like Trent?"

"We think he killed them first . . . quietly. He's been

the biggest 'hero' for a while. They trusted him, right? He probably waited for just the right opportunity, then offed them and got rid of the bodies. Most likely, he picked them off one by one. There weren't *that* many of them, and communication between masked vigilantes has never been great. I'm sorry, but you physical pluses have never been great organizers."

"Well, what about the plus intelligences?"

"They've always been harder to track," he says. "There's no physical characteristic that identifies us. There's not really that many of us to begin with, and the ones that do exist aren't exactly social. Only a few of us are even 'out in the open' . . . and I use that term generously."

"So there's no way of telling how many Trent got to," I say.

"We know of a few whose deaths were always a little . . . suspicious, especially when added to the big picture. The problem is that we don't have any way of finding new plus intelligences, or tracking the ones we know about if they don't want to be found. So, there might be a few who, over the years, contacted Phantom with the hopes that he might mentor them. I'm guessing there's more than a few plus intelligences in shallow graves across the country."

I take a deep breath and rub my eyes. "I don't—Why is he doing this?" I ask.

"The same old reasons . . . money. Power. He had figured out a way to get both, and still be considered a hero. We think he killed off the others to make himself more of a rare commodity. The fewer supers there were, the more in demand he'd be. We also think that as he got closer to thirty-five, he started to get a little desperate . . . He was afraid he'd lose his position as the strongest and the fastest, which would hurt his market position, and the bottom line. His twisted ego wasn't able to handle that . . . any of it."

Jake takes a deep breath. "There's a commonly held belief that serial killers kill because they themselves are trying to cheat death. That's just armchair psychology at best, though."

"And nobody figured this out?" I ask.

"No. Trent spent years setting up his whole 'good guy' image. In the hearts and minds of the public, Phantom Justice was a good guy . . . a dark good guy, but a good guy nonetheless."

I can't help but think of what Allison told me back in school, what feels like a million years ago. "I've spent years being a Goody Two-shoes," she had said. "Years. So now, when I want to do something, I ALWAYS get the benefit of the doubt. Once you have that good girl label, you're set." Trent had proven her theory true, but on a much grander scale.

"So why me?" I ask. "Why'd he help? And keep me alive?"

"Not sure. At first you were part of his wholesome hero image—a cute young sidekick who looked up to him. You pulled in more of the under-ten crowd than he was able to get on his own. You opened up a whole new market for him. But then he realized, even before Allison, that you were becoming a threat. You were too good a person. He knew that if you found out what he was up to, you'd expose him, right?"

"Yeah."

"That's when he started his plan to kill you…and Allison."

Just hearing her name hurts. "But why her? She was no threat to him."

"We think he suspected that she was a triple-plus, and would eventually become a threat to his dominance. She might not . . . but Trent wasn't willing to take that chance. He'd rather just . . . well . . ."

There's an awkward pause.

"We think he'd been looking for an opportunity to kill you two for awhile," he continues. "We think the IGO Computer thing wasn't even that big a concern for him; his main goal was to set up a scenario where he could flush her out and then off you both."

I don't even know how to react to that.

"What he didn't know was that Chaotic started working for us," Jake says.

"When?"

"When he realized what Trent was really up to. The only thing he wanted was to protect his daughter. Needless to say, it didn't work out so well."

"Yeah."

"If Trent is still alive, and we're pretty sure he is, the Feds'll slow him down," Jake says. "But only a little. He's a triple plus. He'll get his hands on whatever he needs."

"He's going to be gunning for me, isn't he?" I ask.

"He's bound to have some nasty surprises. You really should stay put until we can put some kind of plan in place."

"I can't," I say. "I have to do this."

I check the clock on the wall. Six thirty in the p.m. Time to go. I stand up.

"Here," he says, and holds out a brown bag.

I smile. "A lunch?"

"Well, technically a dinner. Take it with you, just in case you decide to be sensible for a change."

I take the bag. "Thanks, Mom." I put my mask on and leap out the window. It's just after dusk, so the air is cold. I barely feel it.

In six minutes, I'm at the train station. I hide in the shadows until the few people waiting board the train. When the doors close, I hop on top of the train. In twenty-five minutes, I'm back in Manhattan. There's a homeless man lying outside the station. I leave the brown bag next to him and continue on my way.

I use my grappling hook to head up to the rooftops.

The city is quiet, just like it has been every other night. Part of me is disappointed, because I could use an outlet for this . . . well, I'm not even sure what to call what I'm feeling: Anger? Anxiousness? Pain? Mix in a little despair, and that comes pretty close. But there hasn't been so much as a purse snatching. And the other part of me is glad for that, because I'm not sure what I'd do to whatever criminal I came across. I'm not sure I could maintain control.

"So why are you out there?" Jake asks the inside of my head.

Before I can think of a disturbing image to force him out of my head, a scream echoes through the night.

"HELP!! Somebody please help me!!"

"That's why," I whisper.

I sprint toward the voice. It's coming from the direction of the river. The buildings are becoming a blur beneath my feet. It's only a few buildings away now. Almost there . . .

"Hold on!" I yell.

"HELP ME!!"

The person screaming is standing with his back to me, on the roof of *the* building . . . Allison's building . . . I stop dead. The Brooklyn Bridge twinkles in the distance. A wave of nausea washes over me.

Monkeywrench turns around to face me, wearing the same outfit from the night in Dr. Chaotic's lab. It's the older one . . . the one that makes it impossible to tell whether Monkeywrench is a he . . . or a she.

"Hello, BB, miss me?"

"That depends," I say. "Who are you?"

"Who do you want me to be?"

I rub my eyes. "I can't do this. Are you Allison, or not?"

Monkeywrench's smile falters. He or she slowly shakes his or her head no.

"Then I don't care who you are," I say. "I'm going home."

"Don't I at least get a thank-you for saving your life?" Monkeywrench asks.

"Fine. Thank you. All set?" I ask. "Great. Then get away from me."

"That may be the most horrible thank-you I've ever gotten."

"Stick around and it'll get worse."

"I want to talk to you."

"Too bad," I say, "because I don't want to talk to you."

"What's your problem?"

"I don't know who you are, but that's someone else's outfit," I growl, "and you don't deserve to wear it."

"Excuse me?"

"You heard me."

"How do you know what I do or don't deserve?" Monkeywrench asks.

"It's simple. The previous Monkeywrench was the most amazing person alive. Unless you were the runner-up, you need to take that costume off."

"No."

I walk toward Monkeywrench. He or she gets into

a fighting stance, but I just keep walking until I'm less than a foot away. I reach for the mask. Monkey knocks my hand away. I reach with the other hand. Monkey knocks my other hand.

"Take it off," I say.

"No," Monkeywrench responds.

"Take it OFF!" I yell, and now I'm grabbing for it. Monkey keeps knocking my hands away. I start punching. He or she starts defending, and I feel like I'm fighting Allison again, and we start getting into a rhythm of punches and kicks and blocks and parries. But this isn't a rhythm I want to get into with a stranger. It was mine and Allison's, and I'm not sharing it with anyone else.

I yell and rush Monkey, hitting him or her square in the stomach. My head is tucked under Monkey's armpit as we hit the ground. I hear the clatter of a mask as it lands on the rooftop and skitters away.

Monkeywrench doesn't move. There's no attempt to push me off and scramble after the mask before I can see. There's no attempt to cover his or her face. He or she is just lying there, waiting for me to look.

So I lift my head up and look.

Allison smiles up at me.

I fall back onto my butt and scoot away from her. My mouth is open. My eyes are filling with tears. My fists are clenched, ready to beat the snot out of her if she's a murderous clone or something.

"I'm not a murderous clone," she says, and smiles. "At least I don't think so. Louis? Am I a murderous clone?"

Louis's voice fills my head. "Indeed you are not, Ms. Mendes."

"Louis?" I ask, looking around.

"You can stop looking around, kid," Louis says. "I'm in your head."

"You're a—?"

"Yup."

"And a—?"

"Yeah, and that too."

I look at Allison "And you're—?"

"Alive? Very much so."

"But the body . . ."

"It was a dummy," she says.

"But I felt it. I held it. It . . . felt like you."

"I know. My father built it for just such an occasion. He cloned my skin for it. Gahh. I can't think about. Gives me the creeps." She shudders.

I look away from her, at the ground, anywhere but her face. I can't process all this. I feel my brain shutting down.

"I know this is a lot to swallow," she says.

"Oh, ya think?"

"I'm really sorry, Scott. This wasn't my idea."

"It was mine," Jake says, also broadcasting in my head, "and if I knew you were going to throw it all away, I wouldn't have bothered."

"Oh great!" I yell. "So are all the plus intelligences out to make me miserable, or just you three?"

"Well, some of us plus intelligences understand the importance of making a plan and sticking to it, even if people get hurt!" Jake yells. "We don't go around tossing away well-thought-out—and successful I might add—plans at the drop of a hat!"

"This is not the drop of a hat!" Allison yells back. She looks at me. "I couldn't do that to you, Scott. Not for another second. It—" She stops. Her eyes tear up. "I can't see you hurt like that."

"He was *supposed* to think you were dead!" Jake yells. "Trent is most likely still alive. And whether Scott likes it or not, they share a past! They have a bond! It's that much easier for Trent to know what Scott is thinking . . . and right now, Scott is practically broadcasting to the world that you're alive!"

"I know," Allison says, and smiles at me. "It's very sweet."

"Sweet is going to get you both killed," Jake says.

"Nonsense," Allison says. "Scott's already faster than him."

"I am?" I ask.

She nods. "Yeah. We think you're going to be even stronger."

"Eventually," Jake yells, "but he's not there yet!"

"Please stop yelling," Louis chimes in. "You're giving me a headache."

"Look," Allison says, "Trent would've figured this whole thing out eventually, anyway. Right?"

No answer.

"Then don't we stand a better chance against him if we're all together?" she asks. "That is, if Scott still wants to be near us." She looks at me, hopeful but wary. "Near me."

She wants me to say I do . . . but I just can't. I'm still reeling. "I . . . it's too much," I say. "I don't know. I just don't know."

She looks disappointed, and that hurts . . . but I barely know what's going on, let alone how I feel about it.

"I understand," she says.

"I have to think about it."

"OK."

"And please . . . all of you . . . get out of my head."

"OK," Jake says.

"All right, kid," Louis says.

"Me, too?" Allison says.

"Especially you," I say.

She's crying now. "I'm sorry, Scott. I'm not sure you'll ever know how much."

"Yeah," I say. "I guess that's another ding against the nonintelligence in the crowd. I'll never know you that well."

"That's not what I meant!"

"So what did you mean?" I yell, because confused or not, I'm angry. "You don't want a little something like lying about your death to get in the way of us trusting each other?"

"Does it have to?" she asks sheepishly.

"It crushed me," I say, barely above a whisper.

"I know."

"Yeah, and that kind of makes it worse. You knew

what it would do to me, and you did it anyway." I walk to the edge of the building. "I need some time."

"I'll be waiting," she says.

"Don't. I don't know how long it's going to take."

Tears are streaming down her cheeks. "Take forever. I'll be waiting."

I give her a solemn nod, then dive off the building. I swing off the fire escape and land silently on one of the window ledges. I stand there, count to "ten Mississippi," then quietly climb back up onto the roof, about a foot from where I dove off. Allison's back is turned to me. I can see her shoulders shaking as she cries.

"OK," I say.

She jumps, startled. She turns around.

"I've thought about it."

"What do you think?" she asks, between sobs.

"I think this sounds kinda dangerous," I say, "and I don't like to do anything too crazy, you know. I'm a pretty levelheaded guy."

I smile at her. She laughs and sprints over to me; I catch her and hold her as tightly as I can without breaking anything.

She looks at me. "You sure you're OK with this?"

"No," I say, "but I don't want to waste any more time

trying to make sense of it. One way or another, it'll work itself out. Right, Louis?"

"Well said, kid."

"Just please," I say quietly, leaning close to Allison's ear, "please don't do that to me again. I can't—"

"I know. I won't."

"Promise."

She puts her hands on the sides of my face and pulls me in and kisses me.

"Will that do?" she asks.

"You know, I'm not sure it will," I say. "I mean that was a pretty traumatic experience. It's going to take something a little more than—"

She grabs me, dips me, plants one on my lips, and holds it.

"Ugh," Jake says. "I'm out."

"You weren't even supposed to be here still," I think.

"All right . . . I'm out, too," Louis says. "Hey, Allison, just be home on time, OK?"

Allison puts one of her thumbs up, but keeps kissing me.

"Atta girl. Hey, kid, don't tire her out too much, got it?"

"It's not him you should worry about," Allison says. Then she throws me off the roof.

"Untraditional way to show affection," I say as I plummet toward the ground.

"That's what you love about me, though, right?" she says, suddenly beside me.

"Who said anything about love?"

"I did." She grabs me, then puts her arm up just in time to grab the fire escape. We swing around, then flip up toward the roof of the next building.

"Which one was that?" she asks as we land.

"We never labeled fire escapes," I say.

"Really?"

"No. Of course, we did. That was FE-212. I just didn't want you to start thinking I was a dork."

"Oh, you don't have to worry about that," she says, laughing. "I've always thought you were a dork."

"Yeah, I figured. Which brings me to my next topic," I say. "If we're going to make a go of this, I think we need some new names. I don't think I want to be Bright Boy anymore."

"Yeah, no kidding. Woof. Plus the words *Monkey-wrench* and *Bright Boy* wouldn't fit on the merchandise."

"Merchandise?" I ask. "And why does your name get to go first?"

"Ooh! I've got it!" she says, pretending like she didn't hear me. "How about The Viper?"

"I like it. Who are you going to be?"

"The Viper."

"Well, then who am I going to be?"

"The Viper's assistant?"

Suddenly, the sound of a man screaming for help echoes in the distance.

"You ready?" I ask.

"Not yet," she says. She takes my hands in hers, then leans in and kisses me. "Now I'm ready."

"Then let's go get 'em."

She leaps off the roof. I follow her.

ACKNOWLEDGMENTS

To Stephen Barbara, who has listened with patience and good humor to my ridiculous ideas and has talked me off many a ledge. DYJ, Stephen, DYJ.

To Susan Van Metre, who responded to my psychic message about wanting to write this book and then provided me with unerring guidance and support. You make the impossible possible, Van Metre! Hee-yah!!!

To Chad W. Beckerman and Joshua Middleton for their patience and for an amazing cover.

To Jason Wells and Laura Mihalick for their endless enthusiasm and tireless efforts.

To Jason Dravis for helping me put some stuff in perspective.

To Trexler, Jody, Davio, Danielle, Emily, Chris, Jef, Jess, John, Aya, Grant, Steve, Justin, Pops, Amanda, and Patrick for their patience and feedback.

To Melissa and Peter, Steve and Sarah, Will and Sara, Joe, Bill, John and Melannie, Lisa (Chica!), Joe and Anita, Chris K., Ryan R., Patti and John, Mike and Dannah, Brad, Paul, and Dorria for their support . . . and for checking in every once in a while to make sure that I was still alive.

To Nonnie, Auntie, Aunt Santella, Uncle Vinny and Linda, Maria and Rob, Will, Jeffrey, Frances, Bachan, Garret and Kerry, Uncle Denny and Donna, Katie, David, Lauren, Ryan, Bobby and Renee, Kristine and Todd, Vincent, Dave and Karina, Jackie, Kim, and the rest of my family for their love and support.

To Laura for always making comics cool. Grab some paper and a stapler and let's make some Wonder Woman boots! To Mom and Dad for their love and faith . . . also for that *sweeeet* Batcave when I was seven, and for never throwing out any of my old comics.

To Emily and Matthew for being amazing . . . and for unintentionally giving me some great ideas for fight scenes.

And finally, to my wife, Teryse, for everything you do to make this possible. Love ya, T.

ABOUT THE AUTHOR

JACK D. FERRAIOLO

grew up in southern Connecticut and cur-
rently lives in northern Massachusetts with
his wife, Teryse; daughter, Emily; and son,
Matthew. He has been writing and editing
for television animation for more than a decade.
He developed, and writes for, *WordGirl* on PBS,
for which he received an Emmy. The *New York
Times* called his first novel, *The Big Splash*,
"entertaining and thrilling" and *Publishers
Weekly* called it "ingenious junior high noir."
Find out more about Jack D. Ferraiolo at
www.jackferraiolo.com.

THIS BOOK WAS ART DIRECTED

and designed by Chad W. Beckerman. The text is set in 12-point Adobe Garamond, a typeface based on those created in the sixteenth century by Claude Garamond. Garamond modeled his typefaces on ones created by Venetian printers at the end of the fifteenth century. The modern version used in this book was designed by Robert Slimbach, who studied Garamond's historic typefaces at the Plantin-Moretus Museum in Antwerp, Belgium.